Don't Never Dead Head

Also by **Thule Taaffe**

Milk and Catfish
available at **PurpleHullPress.com**
or your favorite bookseller

Don't Never Dead Head

A Novel of the Paraclifta Consortium

Thule Taaffe

Purple
Hull
Press

ISBN: 978-1-7353167-3-4

Book and cover design: H. K. Stewart

Purple Hull Press

Printed in the United States of America

To **Todd** and his **wonderful family**

Table of Contents

*I would much rather have men ask me
why I have no statue, than why I have one.*

—Marcus Porcius Cato
Roman soldier and Italian politician (234–149 BC)

Prologue

Spring, 1864
Paraclifta, Arkansas

Nahem Hatfield was a famous PIMP. He was born on a small farm in southwest Arkansas in 1848. The closest town was a settlement called Paraclifta which was located south of the Ouachita Mountains and a few miles east of Oklahoma, which at the time of his birth was known as the Indian Territory.

He spent his formative years working on the family farm and when he turned fourteen, his father ordered him to take a job in the log woods. A couple of years later, the folks in Paraclifta got word that Arkansas had joined the Confederate States of America. They also learned that this had angered the United States and caused a war to break out.

A year or so into this War Between the States, Nahem and the other residents of Paraclifta were unsure about what, if any, duty they might owe to their new government. They heard through the grapevine that a man named Jefferson Davis was their new President and that Arkansas had moved its state capitol from Little Rock to another town. For months the people of Paraclifta patiently waited for instructions or directions from government officials.

In late April, 1864, a traveler informed some of the local residents that there had been several battles around the southern edge of the state in what was described as the Red River Campaign. The traveler also explained that the Confederates were kicking ass and many Arkansas communities had formed their own military units to help support the cause. This news prompted the Paraclifta elders to convene a meeting to determine how their community could assist the Confederacy, especially since things seemed to be going so well for the Rebels.

The only government official in Paraclifta was the county judge, who was responsible for both county roads and the local mail service. The judge, who was thirty-five years old, decided that the typical soldier should be any able-bodied man who was thirty-four or younger. He also suggested that farmers and businessmen be excused from soldiering so that the town's essential services could continue without interruption until the South had beaten back the Yankees.

Based on these guidelines, the town elders concluded that the village of Paraclifta could form a military unit which would provide around a dozen men to the Confederate cause. Since it was already April and the crops were in the field, the county judge further decreed that the local military unit could delay deployment until after the harvest.

Consequently, on November 1, 1864, Nahem Hatfield joined a handful of his neighbors and walked to Paraclifta's very First Baptist Church to report for duty. The county judge declared that these men were the best and brightest lads in the community and he named their unit the Paraclifta Infantry Mens Platoon (PIMP). The elders had previously determined that the unit would be strictly light infantry because the town could not spare any horses or mules.

Nahem and a dozen other volunteers were provided with smart gray jackets which had been sewn for them by the local women. Each jacket was adorned with the unit designation—PIMP—

stitched in large red letters across the left breast pocket. Each of the soldiers was also issued a coonskin cap.

Cognizant that the induction of the men required some sort of formal action, the judge asked them to line up in front of the church, clasp their coonskin caps by the tail, place them over their hearts, raise their right hands and repeat this oath:

> I, *state your name*, do hereby pledge to protect Paraclifta,
> follow my orders and kill Yankees as may be required,
> so help me God.

"I do," the men responded. And after the PIMPs took their oaths, the townsfolk cheered as their boys marched off to war.

Not everyone was excited about sending the PIMPS off to battle. One resident, Ambrose Dalrymple, was troubled by the fact that the unit was composed of thirteen men. Despite his personal trepidation, Ambrose refused to voice his concerns because his patriotism trumped his superstition.

The men from Paraclifta traveled at the rate of about ten miles a day and it took them a week to reach the Red River. One of the soldiers had a juice harp and in the evenings the men would sit around their campfire and sing songs, mostly Baptist hymns or variations thereof. For instance, one of their favorite tunes was, *When the Saints Go Marching In*. The men created their own version of that song which they called, *When the PIMPs Come Marching Home*.

When they finally reached the Red River, the men were out of food. They followed the river south and east for two days but were unable to find a suitable place to cross. The good news was that they were able to fashion some fishing poles which allowed them to stay fed as they wandered the riverbank.

Unable to ford the river, the men decided to travel due east to see if they could find Mississippi. Travel was difficult in frontier Arkansas with only the sun and stars as guides. The men frequently got lost and would sometimes wander around for an entire day only to discover that they had merely traveled in a circle. As the days slipped by, the PIMPs grew weary of beating the bushes.

While the unit roamed aimlessly through the untamed territory, Nahem found himself wishing there was an easier method of land navigation. He wished there was some sort of device he could use to tell him exactly where he was standing and that could provide him with the easiest path to other locations. *It would sure be easier to travel if something like that existed*, he thought. He daydreamed of inventing a tool that would allow him to ascertain his general location, so he could find out where in the world he was located. He decided he would call his device a *General Point Situater*. Then, instead of walking around in circles, the PIMPS could use the GPS to figure out the general area in which they were situated at any given time.

Deep down, he knew there would never be any real need for a GPS because people would simply use a map. And as the men continued their long, circuitous trek through the untamed frontier, he wondered why none of them had thought to bring one.

Throughout their extended cross-state journey, the men dined on whatever varmints they could kill with their rifles and for eighteen days they slogged through the briars and brambles as they headed east and eventually located the Mississippi River. By the time they arrived, they discovered they were out of ammunition. Even worse, they were out of tobacco.

Although they could see the state of Mississippi in the distance, it quickly dawned on the PIMPS that they could never cross that huge river. They had no calendar, but they reckoned they had been marching for over a month. Even though they were devoid of maps or calendars, they still had their homemade fishing poles, so they decided to make camp on the riverbank and fish for a few days. *A few days* turned into two months, but the men made good use of their time.

When they were not fishing or foraging for other food, they trained themselves in military maneuvers with their rifles and practiced loading their guns with imaginary ammunition. They also constructed several crude buildings including a commissary, a mess hall, a post office and *three* Baptist churches. They considered constructing a brothel, but decided against it. Since they had exhausted their tobacco supply, the men smoked cedar bark, muscadine vines, and dried cypress leaves as they fabricated their own small village. When they finished their construction, they called the place: *Pimp Town.*

Another thing the men accomplished at *PIMP Town* was the establishment of a chain of command. They were not exactly sure what to call their commander, but concluded that he should probably be commissioned as a medium-level officer. Thus, they appointed the oldest member of their platoon to serve as their Medium-Captain. The rest of the troops were labeled as sergeants in a descending order of seniority from oldest to youngest: Sergeant First-class, Sergeant Second-Class, and so on. As the youngest member of the platoon, Nahem became Sergeant Twelfth-Class Hatfield.

Nahem was pleased to be promoted to sergeant, but like his comrades, he was tired, hungry and ready to start killing Yankees. Whenever he was not fishing for food or practicing his military moves, he fantasized about what he would do when his unit finally made contact with the rest of the Confederate Army. He imagined himself running up to the closest officer and shouting, "Never fear, the PIMPs are here!"

In early March, 1865, the men decided it was time to break camp. They headed up river to continue their quest to find the Confederate Army. Their last official act before departing *PIMP Town* was to scuttle the post office to alleviate the possibility of any confusion for the Confederate Postal Service. The other buildings were left intact. Sadly, by the date of their departure, *Pimp Town* also had a cemetery because five of the men had succumbed to malaria during the platoon's respite on the riverbank.

When they got moving again, they trudged north on a path that was roughly parallel to the Mississippi. On April 1, 1865, the tired PIMPS wandered into Helena, Arkansas. At that time, the platoon consisted of only the Medium-Captain and Nahem (who had been promoted to Sergeant First-Class) because five of the remaining soldiers had been lost to tetanus, typhoid, diarrhea, and dysentery and one had been left on the trail after contracting a variant of corona virus.

The folks in Helena were excited to see Sergeant First-Class Hatfield and the Medium-Captain and they gave the men a warm welcome. Meanwhile, the local clergy wanted the PIMPs to move off the streets and into a hotel.

Eight days later, around the time when the men had finally regained their strength, they learned that the Rebels had surrendered and the war was over. On the morning of April 11, Nahem and the Medium-Captain sat together on a wooden bench inside the lobby of the grandest hotel in Helena. As the men enjoyed cigarettes, the Medium-Captain explained that he was relinquishing his command and moving to Memphis, Tennessee because he believed that would be a suitable place for a former PIMP to look for work. He gave Nahem command, and asked him to take charge of getting the unit back to Paraclifta.

The next day, newly-promoted, Medium-Captain Nahem Hatfield, the last of the PIMPs, headed back home. The journey required him to travel the entire width of the state, from the Mississippi River almost to Oklahoma, which turned out to be a very long distance.

He made it home forty-three days later, filthy, gaunt and heavily-bearded. The PIMPs never got to fight the Yankees, but they had fought plenty of battles against boredom, briers, disease, hunger, infection, loneliness and spider webs. Even though his unit had never left the state and had never laid eyes on the enemy, Nahem definitely looked like he had survived a war when he finally marched back into Paraclifta.

The people in town had long assumed that all of their PIMPs had been killed in action, so they were ecstatic when they spotted Nahem stumbling down Main Street in his triumphant return. They carried their hero through town on an ox-drawn carriage, presented him with ribbons and pies, and he became the most famous man in the county.

Nahem resumed a quiet life on his family's farm and eventually married the prettiest girl in town. In 1875, he sired a son. Since he had done so little to help the Confederacy during his military career, he decided the least he could do was honor the former President of the Confederate States of America by christening his newborn, *Jefferson Davis Hatfield*.

For the rest of his life, if anyone asked about the war or about how many Yankees he had killed, Nahem would simply look away and say, *I don't want to talk about it* or, *pimpin' ain't easy*. When Nahem died in 1895, he was buried in his gray PIMP uniform and coon-skin cap. He never knew it, but he was the only soldier in Civil War history who had risen through the ranks from Sergeant Twelfth-Class to Medium-Captain.

Nahem's son, Jefferson Davis "J.D" Hatfield, became the County Judge in Paraclifta in 1910. Five years later, the Daughters of the Confederacy underwrote a plan to place a Confederate war statue on the front lawn of the county courthouse. J.D. had no photographs of his father, but he provided a description to a sculptor who created a statue in Nahem's likeness.

The statue was an eighteen-foot tall, Italian marble carving of a Rebel soldier wearing a coonskin hat and holding a musket. An inscription on the base of the monument stated as follows:

This Monument Is Dedicated to the Brave Men of the
Paraclifta Infantry Mens Platoon. We Will Always Remember
the PIMPs' Unselfish Dedication to Their Glorious Cause.
The Principles for Which They Fought Live Eternally.
PIMPin' Ain't Easy.

The statue cost twelve hundred dollars and was dedicated in 1915. The county signed a promissory note to make thirty-dollar payments to the sculptor once a year for the next forty years. The county mailed its first monthly payment on January 5, 1916 but a week later, the payment was returned with a note explaining that the sculptor had died and had no surviving family members. Hence, Paraclifta ended up with the PIMP monument for free.

J.D. Hatfield had never told anyone that his daddy was the PIMP on the pedestal, and for seven decades the memorial stood solemnly on the courthouse lawn where few people even noticed it. The only two folks who paid it any attention were J.D. Hatfield and the guy who mowed the courthouse lawn.

But sixty-seven years later, in March of 1982, an entire region came to know about Paraclifta's Rebel statue when it became a flash-point of controversy.

Day One

1. A Storm Approaches

Sunday, March 7, 1982
3:00 p.m.
Rolling Fork River
Just outside Paraclifta, Arkansas

The two fishermen standing in an oxbow of the Rolling Fork River were relieved when the wind stopped blowing. The breeze which had been nagging them all afternoon, was unseasonably warm and frustrated their ability to cast their lines. The men had waded waist-deep into the river to better reach the bluegill bream in the backwater near the opposite bank. When the wind mercifully stilled, they were standing just a few hundred feet from the exact spot where Nahem Hatfield was born.

The men were wearing work boots and jeans and had entered the river from a rocky shoal that gradually descended into a large pool of clear, blue water. The pool was framed by a thirty-foot bluff of rocks and clay on the opposite side. When the men looked up at the bluff, they felt like ants looking up at a slice of cornbread.

One of the men happened to be staring at the top of the high bank when he noticed dirt and stones tumbling down to the water. Ignoring his fishing rod, he analyzed the disturbance and thought he saw tree roots bolting from the bluff, like arrows being launched from a bow. The roots splashed into the river, surfaced and began slithering about. The frightened fisherman soon realized that the objects were snakes.

As scores of serpents spurted out of the high bank and flopped into the clear pool, one of the terrified anglers yelled to his partner and began to back his way out of the river. The snakes continued to rain from the bluff and soon surrounded the man as he frantically dropped his fishing pole and struggled to sprint to shore. He could hear his companion's splashing, and he prayed they would both be able to extricate themselves from the snaky stream.

Filled with adrenaline, the fisherman was unsure if he had avoided any bites when he finally reached the low bank and rolled onto the rocky shoals. Without taking his eyes off the river, he rapidly arose and shuffled backward, like a prizefighter evading his foe. Even as he executed his escape, snakes continued to cascade from the high bank into the fishing hole. Luckily, the snakes seemed content to stay in the water and did not give chase.

When both men had retreated a safe distance from the river, they plopped down to catch their breaths.

"What on earth is goin' on?" one of them asked.

"Hell if I know," said the other. "But I may never go fishin' again."

And then the men heard a frightening, guttural growl that rolled like thunder. The growl turned into a roar that resembled a jet engine and the sky turned from brown to black. The men looked in the direction of the roar and saw a perfectly-formed funnel cloud directly beyond the river's high bank. They jumped up, sprinted to their truck, and crawled underneath it. From there, they watched an F-3 tornado hurl debris in every direction as it skipped across the river.

The men had been spared by the snakes and the storm, but one of them thought he was having a heart attack and the other began to vomit. While they trembled and gathered their wits, they kept their eyes on the angry tornado as it spun its way due east, directly toward the small town of Paraclifta, Arkansas.

2. How Bad Is It?

The tornado seemed to bounce up and down as it hurtled over dirt roads and bounded along the woods just outside Paraclifta. It skipped off a hill and was well above the ground when it first crossed into the city limits. Then the tip of the funnel twisted back to the ground just west of Main Street. The twister smashed the town's only pharmacy and ripped the roof off one of the filling stations before it skipped up again and cleared the only neighborhood in its path. It officially exited Paraclifta at 3:17 p.m.

Before the clouds had cleared, County Judge Winthrop Hatfield was already in his pickup heading toward the courthouse. Winthrop was the highest-ranking government official in the county and was responsible for the courthouse and all public property. As county judge, he essentially acted as the mayor of the county, but he actually considered himself the *king* of the county.

Winthrop was always one of the most important men in town, but when it came to natural disasters, he was in a league of his own. He always kept his back ramrod straight like a soldier standing at attention. His uniform consisted of a long-sleeved dress shirt tucked into sans-a-belt slacks. The slacks covered his cowboy boots and a cowboy hat always covered his head.

He and his wife had taken shelter in their pantry when they first heard the roar of the storm. Even though his home had been spared and the threat had passed quickly, he feared that his town may have suffered damage. When he arrived at Main Street, he could see the ruins of the pharmacy and he noticed that the downtown filling station looked decapitated. The street was full of limbs, bricks, signs and miscellaneous debris and the air was filled with dust and plastic sacks. *This is bad*, he thought, as he swerved around the obstacles in the roadway.

He drove a block past the damaged buildings and parked on the street in front of the courthouse. He had a reserved parking spot at the back of the courthouse with a sign that said:

> Reserved for Judge Winthrop
> All else will be towed

Rather than wasting any time driving all the way around, he just parked on the street like an ordinary citizen.

He hopped out of his pickup exactly twenty minutes after the storm had plowed through town. He lit a cigarette and strolled toward the destroyed pharmacy. When he was half way there, the town's emergency sirens began to screech. The sirens were mounted on the top corners of the courthouse and were so loud he thought they were going to blow his cowboy hat off his head. *Son of a bitch*, he thought. *It would've been nice if our warning system had kicked on BEFORE the tornado.*

He wished the town had a better way to warn people about dangerous weather. For a moment, he daydreamed about a device that people could keep with them at all times that could instantly alert them to storms or other perils. *That would be very helpful*, he thought. But he could think more about that later; right now, he needed to check the storm damage.

He yelled toward the pharmacy building, "Is anybody in there?!"

He stopped yelling when he realized that nobody would be able to hear him over the screaming sirens. Suddenly he heard more sirens and he looked down the street to see dozens of the town's volunteer fireman flying in his direction. Paraclifta had eighty-six volunteer firemen who had outfitted their personal pickups with emergency lights and sirens. The volunteers were all driving their personal pickups and were traveling single file at a great rate of speed. Obscured by the thick dust wafting through the impact zone, the driver of the lead pickup truck collided with the trunk of a dislodged maple tree which had fallen across his lane of travel. The lead truck skidded to a stop and was hit in the rear by the next truck, which was hit in the rear by the next truck, and so on.

When the last volunteer fireman's vehicle came to a stop, twenty-three trucks had sustained minor damage. Fortunately, all of their sirens continued to work fine and they remained activated as the volunteers emerged from their trucks to start rendering aid to each other.

Winthrop ordered five of the men to begin sifting through the rubble at the pharmacy and sent three others to search the filling station. Another of the volunteers grabbed a chain saw and began to cut the maple tree that had caused the pileup. The remaining volunteers who had not been tasked with official duties stood around and smoked cigarettes.

When the dust settled, the drugstore and filling station were total losses and several residences had suffered minor property damage. A few dozen vehicles, in addition to the volunteers' pickups in the pileup, had also been damaged. But mercifully, Winthrop was confident that no *humans* had been injured by the storm.

As darkness fell, Winthrop walked back to his truck and saw that the courthouse lawn was covered in trash and tree limbs. Two of the ancient catalpa trees that surrounded the courthouse had been sheared in half, but the building itself seemed unaffected.

None of the windows were broken and the power poles and lines looked unharmed. *Boy, were we lucky*, he thought to himself.

Boy, was he wrong. He had failed to take notice of the Confederate memorial on the courthouse square. Had he looked at the statue, he would have discovered that the soldier's coon-skin-hat-clad head was missing.

3. Weaver Looks for Damage

Weaver Gillham was a life-long Paraclifta resident and a retired electrician. He owned fifty-three firearms and, along with his wife, operated the finest, grandest vegetable garden in the county. He was as tall and thin as a full-grown stalk of maize and his head was as bald as a cantaloupe. He always kept himself occupied because he believed that idle hands were the devil's workshop. He was a serious man.

Weaver and his wife were working in their fabulous garden when the storm rumbled through the county. He had lived through many a tornado and could tell by the sound of this one that it had likely inflicted damage on the town. Now that the coast was clear, he decided to drive downtown to see if he could be of any assistance.

When he got to Main Street, he found it blocked by a long line of scrunched-up pickups which caused him to skirt around on the side streets. He observed that the serious damage appeared to be limited to two businesses and plenty of volunteers were already helping with the cleanup, or standing around smoking cigarettes. Satisfied things were under control, he proceeded to circle around the outside of town to avoid driving back through the pickup pile-up.

His return route led him to a gravel road that ran west of town. He was moving slowly so he could be on the lookout for any other storm damage or for any vegetable gardens. He and his wife believed that their garden was second to none and they routinely patrolled the countryside just to make sure.

A few miles down the gravel road, he passed a single mobile home in the edge of a cow pasture. The last he had heard, the home belonged to Junior Smitherton. As he neared the trailer, he noticed that there were several large plants growing out of steel 50-gallon drums in the back yard. This piqued his curiosity and he drove even slower. When he passed by Junior's trailer house, he saw that each plant was overflowing with gorgeous red tomatoes.

He could not believe his eyes. *Junior Smitherton has ripe red tomatoes in early March? What in the hell is going on?* Weaver was bewildered.

Day Two

4. The Consortium Gets Busy

Paraclifta is about two hundred and fifty miles northeast of Dallas, Texas. In 1982, the population of the Dallas-Fort Worth metropolitan area was almost three million and was known as the *Metroplex*. Meanwhile, the greater Paraclifta area had almost three thousand residents and could have been described as the *Backwoodsplex*.

Paraclifta was a town full of meat-eating, gun-owning, church-going people. The men worked hard, paid their debts and enjoyed deer hunting in the fall. Most of them lived in traditional family units. Divorces and single-parent homes were virtually nonexistent. Nobody was on the government dole. Nobody.

John D. Dalrymple was the manager and sole employee of the town's only hardware store. He was fifty-five years old and had short, salt-and-pepper hair and thoughtful brown eyes. He was slender and broad-shouldered and wore blue jeans and pocket tee shirts. He appreciated the comfort of his tee shirts, and he appreciated their design, which allowed him to keep a pack of cigarettes, in close reach, in that handy upper pocket. On workdays,

35

it looked like he had a metal doughnut hanging from his waist, but it was just his copious key collection. In Paraclifta, important men possessed many keys, and they dangled those keys from chains attached to their belt loops. When people saw John D.'s keychain, they knew he was a very important man. What they may not have known was that he was also a very superstitious man.

Every morning, he and a few of his friends would gather in the back of the Paraclifta Hardware store to solve the world's problems. They had calloused hands and redneck tans, and they referred to their group as the *Consortium*. The men would drink coffee and smoke cigarettes as they sat around two industrial cable spools which had been converted to tables. The membership consisted of John D. and four retirees. Their daily sessions started around 6:00 a.m., or whenever they had a quorum. They ended whenever John D. decided it was time to open the store for business.

During their morning sessions, the Consortium's consorts would work their way through discussions about high school football and deer hunting before tackling tougher topics. There were no fraternal organizations, civic clubs or eleemosynary institutions in Paraclifta, so the Consortium filled that void for John D. and his friends. The Consortium had unraveled many mysteries over the years. Among other things, their conjectures had resulted in declarations that the best fruit is the peach, soccer is un-American, men should not wear earrings, mayonnaise is the superior condiment, it would be better to be stabbed than to be shot (if you knew you were going to survive it) and people should not spread rumors.

The men were willing to tackle almost any topic, except politics or religion. They did not believe it was appropriate for polite, reasonable people to sit around and discuss political or spiritual matters. They left those subjects to politicians and preachers, respectively. They also believed that politicians should refrain from preaching and that preachers should steer clear of politics. That was just common sense.

As John D. slid one of his keys into the back door of the hardware store, he knew that this morning's discussion would be focused on yesterday's tornado. He barely had time to get the coffee percolating before the rest of the consorts shuffled in and took their seats in the back of the store. The men always sat in the same spots, just like in church.

In addition to John D., the Consortium's membership included: Weaver Gillham, the gardener; Buddy Wayne Pike, a retired carpenter who had lost three and a half fingers in the line of duty; Evelray Manchester, a retired plumber and huge pro wrestling fan; and Frank "Frogeye" Polk, a retired log truck driver. These consorts considered themselves to be the wisest men in the county. Other people in town considered them to be good old boys. People who met the men for the first time would consider them to be rednecks.

Buddy Wayne wore overalls and the other men wore blue jeans. While John D. wore pocket tee shirts, the others wore untucked flannel shirts. They wore them because they were comfortable and practical. All of them also wore leather, steel-toed work boots because they were men, and that's what men wore.

"Hell of a deal yesterday," said Frogeye. He had jet black hair that was always cut in a flattop and the flattop was always covered by a ball cap. In fact, he had not been outside his house without wearing a hat since October 30, 1980. He also wore forty-eight-year-old, Army-issued, horned-rim glasses that sported the thickest lenses ever engineered by an optometrist.

"Damn sure was," agreed Evelray. "We're dang lucky that nobody got hurt. Nobody."

"I seen that the drugstore and the filling station is all torn up, but how in the hell did all them trucks get smashed up on Main Street?" asked Buddy Wayne.

"They was just respondin' to the emergency when one of 'em smacked into a tree that had done fallen into the road," explained John D.

"That's right," said Evelray. "And also there's a few of them houses back behind the drug store that got some windows busted out and some shingles knocked around.… And them catalpa trees at the courthouse got busted up pretty bad too."

Buddy Wayne was a tree expert and could identify every species of tree in the county. He took a drag on his cigarette and said, "Them toppy trees will be ok. They're tough as a pine knot and they got some deep-ass roots. If some of them inmates can trim off the busted limbs, they'll look good as new next spring."

"I'm just glad we didn't get hit like we did back in nineteen and seventy-five," said Frogeye who was referring to the last tornado to hit the town. Frogeye was an amateur meteorologist and had an extensive collection of journals in which he had logged the daily high and low temperatures and any discernible precipitation over the last 51 years. "What I can't believe is that we didn't get a single drop a rain."

"Surprised it didn't hail," John D. mused.

"I was expectin' some," said Frogeye.

Weaver had been quietly sipping coffee and smoking a cigarette as he listened to the morning's discussion. He leaned back from the table, looked at his colleagues and said, "I hate to get off the subject, but have any of y'all been out by Junior Smitherton's trailer lately?"

"How come?" asked Frogeye, "Did the tornado hit that far outside of town?"

"It ain't unusual for trailers to get tore up when one comes through," added John D.

"Them trailers are like tornado magnets," said Evelray. "Tornadoes generally head straight for them trailer parks."

"I know one thing," said Buddy Wayne, "that Smitherton boy is a doper."

"No, I ain't asking on account of the tornado," continued Weaver. "It's just that I got out driving around after the storm yesterday, and when I went by his place, it looked like he had some tomato plants out back and they already got a bunch of ripe ones on 'em."

Buddy Wayne said, "That don't sound right on a number of counts. First off, the boy ain't got enough ambition to grow a garden. Second, he wouldn't know how to. And, even if somebody planted a garden for his lazy-ass, he wouldn't already have no ripe tomatoes yet."

"That's what I was thinking," Weaver said. "Well, I'll tell you something, I'm aimin' to get to the bottom of it."

During the conversation, Buddy Wayne had decided to switch from cigarettes to snuff. Not forever, but just for the rest of the morning. He had fetched a can of snuff from his overalls and was having difficulty getting it open, mainly because he was missing so many fingers. "Can I bum a pocketknife off somebody?" he asked the group.

Evelray considered making a snide observation about a man being in public without a pocketknife, but he let it go. Instead, he fished out his own pocketknife, opened the blade and gently slid it to Buddy Wayne without comment. Buddy Wayne snatched up the knife and used the tip of the blade to circle the lid of his snuff can. Then he closed the knife and slid it back to Evelray.

John D., who had been watching this operation, made an urgent observation. "Hold on just a minute, Buddy Wayne. You need to open that knife back up before you give it back. You *always* return a pocketknife to somebody in the same condition as when you received it. You're puttin' Evelray at great risk by closing a knife that *he* opened."

"He's right," said Frogeye. "That right there is bad luck."

Buddy Wayne resented John D.'s chastising. He felt like a scolded child. He unceremoniously retrieved the knife, re-opened the blade and re-slid it to Evelray. Crisis averted.

"Much obliged," said Evelray, who was swaying from side to side scraping his shoulders against the backrest of his metal chair. He followed that up by slinking his arm through the collar of his flannel shirt and using his fingers to claw at the skin between his shoulder blades. Despite contorting his entire upper body, he managed to keep his lit cigarette perfectly balanced in the right corner of his mouth.

"What the hell is wrong with you?" asked John D.

"I got a terrible itch that I can't reach.... I'd ask one of y'all to scratch it fer me, except that I'm a full-grown man." Evelray stopped his futile scratching strategy and looked at John D. "Reckon what in this here hardware store would be the best thing to use as a back scratcher?"

John D. put his mind to work. It subconsciously scrolled through the entirety of the store's inventory. He felt like a ghost floating up and down every aisle, surveying the full array of its retail goods. Finally, he nodded and said, "How 'bout a standard, twelve-inch dowel rod. They're long and light."

Buddy Wayne, the retired carpenter, disagreed. "Yeah, but you wouldn't get a lot a surface area. And, you'd be liable to snap it in half. I'd use the claw side of a regular claw-hammer. That'd do the trick."

"They're mighty heavy," said Evelray.

Buddy Wayne was indignant. "Not if you get used to slinging one for 40 years. But I guess if a regular hammer is too much fer you to handle, you could always get yourself one a them little ball-peen hammers."

Weaver, the retired electrician, offered another alternative. "Get yourself some half-inch, flexible metal conduit," he suggested. "It's light and you can bend it 'round all sorts a ways."

Frogeye, the retired truck driver, decided to chime in. "It's simple. What you need is a standard coat hanger. Just straighten it all the way out and bend the end sideways. You can reach any spot on the human body with that, and you can come at it from damn near any angle."

"Well, coat hangers is one of the few things we don't sell in here," John D. pointed out. "So that answer is disqualified."

"Oh," muttered Frogeye in defeat.

The men wrangled with this topic for another half hour and it turned out to be one of the rare instances where the Consortium was unable to reach a consensus. The debate ended in a stalemate.

"I reckon you're about to get busy," Weaver said to John D. "Folks gonna be in here all day gettin' stuff for repairs."

"That's a fact." said John D.

Buddy Wayne spit some tobacco juice into his empty Styrofoam coffee cup. "I reckon I'm gonna go lend a hand with whoever needs some carpenter work," he announced.

Retirement had never prevented Buddy Wayne or anyone else in Paraclifta from lending a helping hand. The members of the Consortium had spent their lives performing menial work for fair wages. They were honest, God-fearing men and the notion of treating someone unfairly had never crossed their minds.

"I reckon Evelray's right. It's fixin' to get busy 'round here so I'd better get the store opened up," said John D. Then he looked at his friends as said, "Y'all let me know if anybody needs anything."

And with that the Consortium adjourned.

5. Finius Kochran, Big-time Legislator.

10:00 a.m.
Office of Finius Kochran
Washington, D.C.

Paraclifta was one of dozens of small communities located within the South Arkansas Congressional District. Finius Kochran was the district's long-time Congressman. He was 63 and had a body that looked like it belonged behind a big desk. He had a large beer belly that he covered up with expensive suits. He was clean-shaven with brushy orange hair and he looked like a grouchy cartoon character. He was about as charming as an ironwood stump and was the kind of person who had never considered reading a novel. Even though he hated reading, he loved to wear reading glasses because he thought it made him look smarter.

Finius had made a name for himself by being one of the most boisterous big-mouths in Congress. His strategy was simple: he fought for his financial supporters and opposed anything and everyone else. He seldom voiced an opinion on issues that would not promote his re-election or directly benefit his benefactors. His political philosophy was simple: *do anything necessary to get reelected.* He called himself a conservative because it was easy and sounded respectable, but as a rule, he just opposed anything that might not directly help his friends. He had learned that when he helped his friends, they helped him back. He was a master of intellectual debate and whenever someone disagreed with his position, he would simply call them a communist.

Finius's mother had worked as a cobbler. After he became a congressman, he had done great work for the Society of Cobblers and Merchants (SCAM). He was especially proud of his support for the Economic Recovery Tax Act of 1981, which drastically reduced the marginal income tax rate. The only reason he had ever run for Congress in the first place was that some corporate executives had assured him that they could get him elected. Those executives were now celebrating the new tax laws which had dramatically increased their incomes. Because of these tax cuts, the executives did not have to increase their own paychecks in order to take home more money. Instead, they just paid less in taxes. Once they had all that extra money, they could spend it on things like yachts and second homes to help *stimulate* the economy. The scheme worked like magic. It was officially known as *trickle down economics*.

Finius had grown up playing with the wooden foot forms that his mother had used to craft shoes. The forms were called shoe-lasts and he had engraved his name on one of them which he kept on his desk in Washington. The week after the Economic Recovery Tax Act of 1981 became the law of the land, some of his financial supporters paid him a surprise visit and presented him with a new shoe-last just like the one they had seen on his desk, except the new shoe-last was plated in 24 carat gold. It also contained an engraving which looked like this:

To our dear friend,
Congre$$man Finiu$ Kochran
—*Don't be a communist*—

Finius loved the golden shoe-last so much that he trashed the authentic one he had inherited from his mother. It was an easy decision for Finius because he believed that gold always trumped family. His new gold shoe-last was heavy, smooth and shiny, and he was extremely proud to have it on his desk.

Whenever he was not concentrating on helping his friends or calling people communists, he liked to stare at the golden foot-form and focus on ways that he could gin up positive publicity for himself. Even though he loved Washington and detested visiting his home district, he had learned that a sure-fire way to get positive press was to show up at the scene of a disaster.

As luck would have it, he was pleased to learn that a tornado had touched down in Paraclifta yesterday.

As he fondled his golden shoe-last, he yelled at one of his secretaries, "Call up Paraclifta and get me Judge Hatfield on the phone! ... And line me up some airline tickets to Little Rock."

"Yes sir," said the secretary. "And sir, I've got PMS."

Finius had forgotten that he had ordered someone to get the executive director of the Plastic Manufacturers' Society on the phone. PMS represented all the stalwarts of the petroleum and plastics industry and it had become one his most generous contributors. He was always looking for ways to help his friends at PMS.

"What're you waiting for," he shrieked, "Patch 'em through!"

Why do I have a staff full of idiots, he asked himself. *Ignoring PMS? It's no wonder I have headaches, cramps and stress all the time.*

His staff eventually got the call directed to his office telephone. The director informed Finius that PMS was still working on its *plastic proliferation project.* Two years earlier, Finius had helped PMS work to convince department stores and super-markets to swap paper bags with plastic sacks. Now, he learned that PMS had partnered with industrial soapers to start marketing liquid hand soap. The liquid soap had a higher profit margin than traditional bars of soap, and more importantly, it would be sold in plastic dispensers.

After hearing the pitch, Finius reported that he was *all in*. "I'll do anything I can to help with PMS," he told the director.

It was shaping up to be a good week, a prime opportunity for some well-deserved publicity coupled with a chance to help out one of his biggest supporters. A smile spread across Finius' face as he stared at his gold-plated foot form.

6. Cammack Cafflin, Part-time Legislator.

The Arkansas legislative branch was known as the General Assembly. Every odd-numbered year, the General Assembly would convene at the State Capitol while the rest of the citizenry hunkered down and hoped for the best. State Representatives from small communities in every corner of the state would travel to Little Rock for the legislative session. The General Assembly was like the most exclusive deer camp in a state that was full of deer camps.

Since the actual job of passing new laws took only a few weeks every other year, most of the state representatives were content to show up at the biennial sessions, vote on a few bills, collect their paychecks, and then go back to their real jobs and families. But a few of them, like State Representative Cammack Caflin, enjoyed legislating so much that they wanted to do it full time.

Cammack represented the district that included Paraclifta, but he lived in a town that was 40 miles to the south which was called Paraloma. He had a vacant stare and a perpetual odd look on his face. He was the kind of man who looked, and acted, like he had an imaginary friend. He enjoyed being a legislator and he loved going to Little Rock as often as possible. He ran a small insurance agency which had two secretaries who could easily run the business without his assistance. All they really had to do was collect monthly premium payments from their customers and then mail those payments to big insurance companies in places like Chicago and Omaha.

Serving in a government position made Cammack feel very important and he was always looking for reasons to drive up to Little Rock for meetings and conferences. He was unopposed in his first election and after he took office, he called Congressman Finius Kochran to seek his advice.

"Congressman, I know you're up at the federal level," he said to Finius, "but I just got elected to the state legislature and I've got a lot of really good ideas."

Here's what Finius told him: "Son, if you wanna work on *ideas*, then you need to become a scientist. As a state legislator, all you need to do is keep your mouth shut, vote on the budget every other year and then get your ass back home. Every once in a while, you might consider drawing up a law to deal with whatever y'all need down there in the boondocks, like how to sell firewood or how to handle dope smokers. But leave the serious law-making to us professionals up here in Washington."

Cammack had been disappointed by that advice. He had been a state representative for four terms and had never introduced any legislation. Despite Congressman Kochran's counsel, he still hoped that someday he could get the nerve to write up his own law.

Even if he could not craft some legislation, he knew that he needed to stay in touch with the local officials in his district. Since everyone in the state had heard about the Paraclifta twister, he decided he needed to drive up there to visit with the county judge. *It won't be as fun as a trip to the State Capitol, but maybe I can get reimbursed for my mileage*, he thought.

7. The Great Tomato Caper

Weaver Gillham was sitting at home fretting about Junior Smitherton's tomato plants.

Weaver had lived in Paraclifta his entire life, except for a spell in the Army where he had been trained as an *eleven bravo*, a basic infantry rifleman. After his military tour, he returned home and learned to be an electrician. That kept him occupied until he retired at age sixty and took up gardening. While he had been a decent soldier and an above-average electrician, he ultimately became an expert gardener and his vegetable production had increased exponentially every year. He and his wife raised almost anything that could grow in the fertile Paraclifta soil, except for carrots. Weaver refused to grow a carrot. He handled the planting and picking and his wife handled the cooking and canning. When they were not managing their own vegetable patch, they were keeping a close eye on everybody else's.

Junior Smitherton was not known as a gardener. He had never worked and he rarely ventured out from his mobile home. Weaver was still mystified about the bushy green plants he had seen behind Junior's trailer— plants which appeared to be covered in ripe red tomatoes.

Weaver knew it was entirely too early for ripe tomatoes. He had never even *planted* tomatoes before mid-April, much less produced a ripe one. Junior's place did not have a greenhouse and there was no plausible explanation for how he could already have ripened tomatoes. It was a mystery that Weaver was compelled to unravel.

As an infantry rifleman, he knew how to plan and execute a clandestine reconnoiter and surveillance operation. After it turned full dark, he put on his camouflage hunting jacket, grabbed a pack of cigarettes and one of his 53 firearms, and aimed his pickup toward Junior's trailer.

He drove a half mile past the trailer, parked his truck on the shoulder of the gravel road, and popped the hood. In order to avoid any suspicion, he could now claim that he had stopped because of engine trouble. He lit a cigarette and walked back toward the trailer to take a quick look around. When he got close, he saw the neon green hue of a television screen through the front windows. No outside lights were burning and there was no indication that Junior had a dog, so he quietly eased around to the back yard to make a close-up examination of the magical tomato plants.

The plants were about head high with wide exotic leaves. He grabbed one of the red fruits and discovered that it was nothing more than a Christmas ornament, the same kind of red balls that his wife hung on their tree during the holidays. *What in the heck?* he wondered. Suddenly the back door of the trailer opened and spilled light into the pasture. Weaver dashed behind one of the bushes while a glassy-eyed boy wearing nothing but a dingy pair of underpants stepped out, looked from side to side and then returned to the trailer and closed the door. Weaver was back on the move the moment the door closed.

During his tactical exfiltration, he thought back to his infantry training and the instructions for conducting a successful reconnaissance and surveillance operation. A small group of six to eight men would be tasked to reconnoiter an enemy position. After getting as close as possible to the objective, two soldiers, serving as scouts, would slowly and stealthily belly crawl until they could see the target from different vantage points. The scouts would make a careful observation of anything and everything in their line of sight before crawling back to the rest of their party. Upon their return, the scouts would report *everything* they had seen without sparing any detail. The purpose for this was simple: once all of them were in possession of the complete details of the scouts' observations, that information would not be lost as long as one of the soldiers made it back alive.

Even after transitioning back to civilian life, Weaver had frequently thought about that training. He believed that everyone had an obligation to share crucial information as soon as possible, because you never know if you are going to make it back alive. Consequently, when he made it home, he provided his wife with a full briefing of his operation.

"I ain't sure what he's growing, but it ain't tomatoes," he told her. "Whatever's happenin' behind that trailer, we ain't being out-gardened by Junior Smitherton."

While she was glad that the expedition had not uncovered anything that would impugn their garden's reputation, she still encouraged him to share his findings with the county sheriff.

"That's exactly what I aim to do," he replied.

Day Three

8. Tomatoes and Cigarettes

Tuesday, March 9, 1982

5:57 a.m.

Paraclifta Hardware

Paraclifta, Arkansas

The members of the Consortium were in their regular seats in the back of Paraclifta Hardware. They were drinking coffee, smoking cigarettes and discussing the recent tornado damage.

"Several of them houses a block east of Main Street got busted up pretty bad," Buddy Wayne reported. "I helped get some windows boarded up and we got some tarps over some of 'em that are gonna need roof work."

Evelray said, "I heard they're gonna set up a trailer house on the edge of town for the pharmacy to work out of 'til they can rebuild the store."

Buddy Wayne nodded. "That's good news," he said. "I gotta have some place to pick up them heart pills they got me on."

"Speaking of trailers, let me tell y'all what I found out at Junior Smitherton's place," said Weaver. "I went out there last night to check on them plants which I thought was tomatoes. Turns out they ain't tomatoes. They're just bushes that he stuck Christmas balls on to. It made 'em look like tomatoes, but I knew it couldn't a been, cause it's way too early."

"Why in the world was he decorating bushes?" wondered Evelray.

"Ain't no telling," said Buddy Wayne, "but I done told y'all he's a doper."

"Well thank goodness he ain't beatin' you at tomato-growing," chuckled Frogeye. "That's the most important thing."

"Yeah. But it's still a weird deal," said Weaver.

Buddy Wayne reached into the breast pocket of his denim overalls to fetch a cigarette. He pulled out his cigarette pack only to find it empty. He was also out of snuff. He wadded up the empty cigarette package, dropped it on the cable-spool table and turned to Evelray. "Can I bum a smoke?"

Evelray tossed him a cigarette. "You know something, I wish I lived in a world where you could just walk around and go up to somebody and say, *hey, can I bum a smoke?* And then they'd just hand you a cigarette. For free. And you could just always have free cigarettes all the time."

Buddy Wayne frowned and then tossed the cigarette back to Evelray. "Forget it," he said.

"I was just joshing," Evelray said.

Frogeye ignored his friends' childish behavior. "The truly good news is that the dang tornado didn't hurt nobody."

"Nobody," said Weaver. "It's a real miracle. It weren't near as bad as that one back in '75."

"Reckon how come they always name hurricanes, but not tornadoes?" asked John D.

"That's a good question. Prob'ly 'cause people on the East Coast think they're better than everybody else," Frogeye suggested. "If we was gonna name the one that hit here on Sunday, reckon what we'd name it?"

"How about Tornado Junior?" Suggested Evelray.

"How come?" asked John D.

Evelray blew a stream of cigarette smoke toward the ceiling. "On account of the fact that it destroyed the drug store and Junior Smitherton is a druggie," he answered.

The other men laughed. "That actually makes sense," agreed Weaver.

Frogeye changed the subject. "I know that storm was terrible, but I got some bad news personally, I seen a big deer on my way up here this morning."

"How's that bad news?" asked Buddy Wayne.

"Well," Frogeye explained, "you only get a certain number of deer *sightings* in any given year. You want them sightings to take place whilst you're in the deer woods with your rifle. You don't want to have one wasted while you're drivin' into town in the springtime."

John D. balanced his cigarette on the edge of an ashtray and considered Frogeye's *sightings* pronouncement. *That makes perfect sense,* he thought. *Of course you have a finite number of sightings. The key is for the sighting to occur at the right time.*

"Well, I need to go out and see if I can help some people," Buddy Wayne said. Then he looked at Evelray and said, "*After* I go buy some smokes."

The other men stubbed out their cigarettes and John D. headed up front to open the hardware store for business. The Consortium was adjourned.

9. Weaver Calls the Law

Arlen Dingler was the law in Paraclifta. He was a steadfast and serious lawman. He was hatchet-faced with a wide brown handlebar mustache. Just like the county judge, he wore a cowboy hat every single day. He was six feet tall and looked like a linebacker, which is the position he had played for the Paraclifta Hornets. He had taken a job with the sheriff's office right out of high school and had been the heir-apparent when the man who hired him took retirement. He had a no-nonsense attitude, was devoted to his job, and was dedicated to keeping the peace.

Since he served in an elected position, he had ordered his deputies not to write speeding tickets. If they caught a speeder, they were to issue the scofflaw a tongue-lashing and then let him off with a warning. That way, people would slow down, but Arlen would not worry about losing any votes.

The local justice system spanned three stories in the county courthouse. The jail was in the basement and the courtroom was on the second floor. The sheriff's office was sandwiched in between on the ground level of the building.

Arlen wore blue jeans, pointy-toe cowboy boots and starched denim shirts with button-down pockets. He wore a shiny gold star on his left pocket and kept a shiny silver revolver in a holster attached to the right side of his belt. He had six deputies who all looked and dressed the same. His men wore long-sleeved beige-colored shirts and blue jeans with black leather belts. Their belts held pistols on one side and walkie-talkies on the other. They all wore black baseball caps with the word LAW in gold lettering over the top of the bill. Because they were good-mannered, they always removed their service caps when they were indoors.

The deputies had been working overtime as a result of the weekend tornado and Arlen was sitting in his office filling out payroll documents when he was interrupted by a call from Weaver Gillham.

"Hey, Weaver," Arlen said, "how's the garden coming along?"

"So far, so good. I'm real glad that nobody was hurt by that tornado but I shore wish we'd a gotten some rain out of it," replied Weaver.

"I heard that," said Arlen. "Well, what can I do for you?"

"Well … this is kinda weird, but I felt like I needed to give you a call. I was out by Junior Smitherton's place the other day and there's something strange goin' on."

Arlen was not surprised. "We've had our eyes on him for a spell. What's the deal?"

"Well …. it looked like he had some tomatoes in his back yard, so, I ain't gonna lie, I walked back there to look, and they ain't tomato plants. They're just shrubs but he's got red Christmas balls hangin off of 'em."

"Is that right?" Arlen asked. "That sounds like something I need to get somebody to take a look at."

"OK. I just wanted to let you know."

"I appreciate it Weaver. I'll let you know what we find out and don't forget about me when them purple-hull peas get ready." Arlen loved purple-hull peas, and nobody grew them better than Weaver. Nobody.

"Will do," said Weaver.

10. Dicey Discovers the Decapitation

Dicey Davidson was twenty-seven years old but had the mental acuity of a third-grader. He was a strong, good-natured boy who had never been quite right. His mental deficiencies had never been officially diagnosed, but his mother had encountered difficulties while she was pregnant and eventually had a dicey delivery.

The men of the Consortium took care of Dicey and often asked him to help with odd jobs. Dicey had become fascinated with measuring things after Buddy Wayne had taught him how to read a tape measure. Since then, Dicey always had a large tape measure strapped to his belt and he wandered around town making miscellaneous measurements. Because of his limited mental capacity, he was only able to identify lengths to the closest half inch. The smaller fractional markings on the tape were beyond his grasp.

For the first few hours of the morning, Dicey had been helping the volunteer firemen drag limbs out of Main Street. While the men were amazed at Dicey's strength, they were annoyed by the fact that each time he slid a limb from the street, he would take an additional five minutes to measure it and then shout out the results. After heaving

59

one of the larger limbs on the sidewalk, Dicey circled it three times and then yelled, "Eleven feet, three inches and four of them little notches!"

Once all of the limbs had finally been removed from Main Street, one of the volunteer firemen suggested that Dicey should go to the courthouse and start dragging the limbs littering the courthouse lawn into a single pile. Dicey was happy to oblige after being assured that he could continue reporting his measurements.

He slapped his professional, stainless-steel retractable tape measure back onto his belt and ambled up to the courthouse lawn. While he was surveying the scene to figure out which broken limb to grab first, his eyes landed on the Rebel soldier statue. *Wait a second,* Dicey thought, *there ain't no head on that man.*

Gertie Fitzhugh happened to be walking by the courthouse at the same time. Gertie was an elderly woman who was known in town as the *Chinquapin Lady* because she always carried a box made of chinquapin oak that contained a burial shroud she had designed for her funeral. When chinquapin oak burns, it produces raucous popping and gyrating sparks and she made it a point to tell people:

> When I drop dead put me in a chinquapin coffin,
>   that way I can go through hell just a poppin'.

She wanted everyone to know that whenever she dropped graveyard dead, she was to be cloaked in her black shroud *and* buried in a chinquapin coffin.

She could tell that Dicey was addled. "What are you lookin' at?" she asked.

Dicey pointed toward the statue and said, "That man ain't got no head."

The Chinquapin Lady turned to the statue and saw the decapitated Rebel soldier. "Oh my Lord!" she shrieked. "What an unspeakable catastrophe. ... Thank goodness I've got my burial box because I might just drop graveyard dead!"

11. The Chinquapin Lady Breaks the News

The Chinquapin Lady had never paid much attention to the Rebel soldier statue, but she was a member of the Daughters of the Confederacy and proud of the role her family had played in the Civil War. As a little girl, she had heard many tales about her family's service. One of her favorite stories involved her great-aunt, Millicent Hempstead.

Millicent was a young woman when news reached Paraclifta that Arkansas was at war. She was a renowned seamstress and was one of the women who had designed the uniforms that were presented to the PIMPs. While Millicent was working on Nahem Hatfield's jacket, she had accidentally dropped the spool of red thread she was using to stitch the PIMP logo. The spool skittered across the floor of her log cabin and landed near her pet kitten, which started batting the spool around as a toy. Millicent giggled as he pawed at the spool and caught it with his mouth. After a few minutes of play, she pried the spool from the kitten's mouth and returned to her sewing.

After reclaiming the spool, Millicent stretched out a section of line as long as her arm and used her teeth to snip the thread. She repeated this process until she had completed stitching the PIMP logo onto the breast of Nahem's gray jacket. Several days later, her kitten became vicious and eventually died after suffering a series of violent seizures. Three weeks later, Millicent took ill. At first she became lethargic and lost her appetite, and then she began to shake and convulse. She never recovered, and died a few days later. Her family presumed that the kitten had carried rabies, a zoonotic disease that could be transmitted from animals to humans, and that Millicent had been infected by the contaminated spool of thread. If the family's theory was correct, it meant that when Millicent died, a month before the PIMPs began their march, she became the town's first war casualty.

The Chinquapin Lady had grown up hearing about her great-aunt's sacrifice. She thought that Millicent deserved her own monument on the courthouse lawn. She never knew that the soldier on the statue was the same man who had ended up with the very jacket her great-aunt had sewn. All she knew at this very moment was that she needed to notify the county judge about the desecrated memorial.

The Chinquapin Lady stowed her burial box under her left armpit and walked into the county judge's office. Judge Hatfield had two young secretaries named DeeDee and Dorinda. DeeDee was white, tall and skinny. Dorinda was black, short and full-figured. Everyone in the courthouse called Dorinda "D" and called DeeDee, "Double D." This was somewhat amusing because Dorinda was the one who actually looked more like a *Double D*.

DeeDee was the first to greet the Chinquapin Lady.

"Hello, Miss Gertie," she said.

"Hi there Double-D," the Chinquapin Lady replied. "Is the judge around?"

"He shore is," said Double-D, pointing to the back office. "You can go on in there."

The Chinquapin Lady marched into Winthrop's office. He was staring out at the storm debris across the courthouse lawn.

"Judge, we got a major situation," said the Chinquapin Lady. "You better sit down."

The last time the Chinquapin Lady had told the Judge *we got a major situation* it had been because the town had become littered with plastic sacks. The yellow sacks had been stuck to trees, road signs and fence posts all over town and the Chinquapin Lady had warned him that if they were not cleaned up quickly, she was liable to drop graveyard dead. As Winthrop sat down behind his desk, he was expecting to hear another trivial complaint. He decided to make sure that the Chinquapin Lady knew he was already dealing with a *major situation* and then maybe she would take her complaint to someone else.

"I reckon we do have a major situation, ma'am. It looks like a bomb exploded and destroyed about a third of our business district. We've lost our only drugstore and half of our service stations. Lots of our neighbors have got house problems on account of that terrible storm. Most of the volunteer firemen wrecked their pickups and we ain't got enough money in the budget to pay all the overtime that we owe to the sheriff's office. On top of that, it looks like a scad of drunk loggers have done taken chain saws to the trees on our beautiful courthouse lawn. … But what do you need to tell me about?"

Unfazed by the Judge's disaster recitations, the Chinquapin Lady furrowed her brow, leaned forward, and dramatically explained the reason for her visit.

"Well, everything you said is bad, I can't deny it. But apparently, you ain't taken a *real good look* outside around the courthouse. Our pride and joy, the great Confederate statue, just in front of this very building, has been desecrated. The soldier, one of our very own PIMPs, has done lost his head! It's a flat-out disgrace is what it is, and if it ain't fixed quick, I'm afraid I might drop graveyard dead."

"What in the world are you talking about?' asked Winthrop.

The Chinquapin Lady pointed to the front of the courthouse. "I'm talking about that brave Rebel soldier out there. His head got lopped off in the storm."

Winthrop rose from his chair, walked to the window in the corner of his office and stood ramrod straight as he looked out at the statue. Then he slowly turned around and faced the Chinquapin Lady.

"Oh dear," he said. "What are we gonna do?"

"We gotta fix that PIMP," she said. "He's gotta have a head."

12. The Judge Asks for Help with the Head

11:30 a.m.
Office of Judge Winthrop Hatfield
Paraclifta, Arkansas

Judge Hatfield was disappointed about the missing head, but he was not as upset as the Chinquapin Lady. To him, this was just another problem that had been dropped in his lap. He was more worried about the loss of two local businesses, the damage to private residences and public property and the catalpa limbs that were still scattered all over the courthouse lawn. To make matters worse, his congressman was planning to tour the damage tomorrow and that would bring a hoard of media coverage.

The judge secretly wanted to become a congressman himself, but he knew he did not have the name-recognition or resources to take on Finius Kochran. That meant he had to keep kissing up to Finius for the time being. He knew Finius was usually able to procure federal funds to help Paraclifta from time to time. *Maybe he can get us some money to help fix the statue,* he thought. *Heaven knows we ain't got the money in the budget for a new one.*

He decided to give Finius a call.

"Congressman Finius Kochran's office," said the receptionist.

"This is Judge Winthrop Hatfield calling for the congressman," he said.

A moment later, Finius was on the phone.

"Hell of a storm down there, Judge," he said, "glad nobody got hurt. Nobody."

"We were blessed. That's for sure," answered Winthrop.

"Well, I'll be down there around lunch tomorrow to take a look around. I'd like to do like we did back in '75, so have the sheriff ready to shut down the area so we can get in there with some TV people. See if you can find me some regular folks who'll look good enough for TV so I can shake hands with 'em and talk to 'em for a few minutes."

"Will do," said Winthrop.

"Good," said Finius. "What're you gonna need help with, besides free money?"

"Well, I reckon we just need whatever assistance y'all can get us but I may also need help with something out of the ordinary," Winthrop replied. "The Confederate statue at the courthouse got some damage."

"In what way?" asked Finius.

"Well, it looks like that the soldier's head got knocked off."

"Just put the damn thing back on it then," Finius suggested.

"We would, but it's gone. I reckon we'll need a new one."

"Well, that's a first. I ain't never had nobody ask me to help with a head. Nobody," Finius chuckled. "But I'll see what I can do, and I'll see you tomorrow."

"Thanks," said Winthrop. *Maybe that'll take care of that*, he thought.

(CHAPTER THIRTEEN has been removed at the request of
John D. Dalrymple)

14. Weaver Gets a Call from the Law

Sheriff Dingler's deputies patrolled only during daylight hours. A typical patrol required a deputy to drive through downtown a few times and then roam around on the county roads. It also involved a fair share of cigarette breaks and visiting with citizens. Arlen saw no reason to schedule any regular night patrols because there would be nothing for his deputies to do and everyone in town would be asleep anyway. At the end of their shifts, his deputies were obliged to come by the office to give him a quick update. He preferred oral reports because he and his deputies hated paperwork.

Arlen was about to make some phone calls when one of his deputies came in to provide an end-of-shift report.

"Not much going on today, Sheriff. Not much traffic and lots of folks still helping with the storm cleanup. I did make one traffic stop."

You better not've written a ticket, thought Arlen. He looked at the deputy and said, "Tell me about it."

"Well, I was parked over by the barber shop and a Buick Skylark, red in color, came creeping down Main Street and it had somebody standing on the hood."

Arlen's eyebrows arched quizzically. "Tell me more," he said.

"Well, I pulled 'em over and it turns out it was one of Frogeye's nephews, the one that plays on the offensive line."

"Oh," said Arlen.

"He needed a ride to school and when his buddy pulled up at his house, he decided to stand on the hood to work on his balance. He called it hood-surfing."

Arlen nodded his head. "How'd you handle it?"

"I told 'em that wasn't a good idea in the middle of town. I said that there's plenty of dirt roads out in the county where they could do that shit."

"Good," said Arlen. "Anything else to report?"

"Only that the Chinquapin Lady was stumblin' around by the East End Diner mumbling about headless PIMPs. She wasn't really causin' no problem, but I think she may be gettin' even crazier than usual."

"That's a big 10-4," said Arlen, using the police's numerical code for *yes*. "We're gonna just have to keep an eye on her. Thanks for the report and I'll see ya' tomorrow."

Arlen picked up his telephone and was dialing Weaver's number as the deputy took his leave.

"Hello," answered Weaver.

"Them plants at Junior's trailer house was marijuana," the sheriff told him. "Thanks to you we arrested his ass."

"Well, I just thought it was suspicious."

"Junior thought he could disguise 'em as tomato plants by decorating 'em with them Christmas balls. It's a good thing you reported it."

"Reckon what's gonna happen to him?" Weaver asked.

The sheriff: "Well, since he was growing plants, that's what we call *manufacturing*. He's looking at about forty years."

"Damn," said Weaver.

"That's what happens to dopers," said the sheriff. "That marijuana is killin' people and it's ruining this country. There ain't no place for it."

"I guess that's right."

"And listen, Weaver, have you ever thought about being a deputy?"

"I appreciate it," Weaver replied. "But I reckon my garden keeps me busy enough."

15. The Judge Talks to the Law

With his back as straight as a pool cue, Judge Hatfield descended one flight of courthouse stairs and walked into the Sheriff's Office.

"Where's Arlen?" he asked.

A deputy pointed down the hall. Winthrop strode down it until he found the sheriff in the break room. Arlen was crouched beside the department's new copying machine, placing sheets of paper into one of the trays.

"Arlen," Winthrop announced, "I need you and your boys to be on the lookout for a missing head."

Arlen looked up from the end of the copying machine. "Do what?" he asked.

"Our monument got hit in the storm. That Rebel soldier's head came off."

Arlen nodded. "That explains a lot. ... I just got a report that the Chinquapin Lady was upset about a headless PIMP. Maybe she's not gettin' crazier after all."

"She's the one who reported it," Winthrop confirmed. "But she *is* getting crazier. Anyway, the head's missing and I need y'all to be on the lookout for it."

"OK, but I've done got guys committed to handlin' traffic and keepin' watch over the storm-damaged areas and I happen to be workin' on the biggest drug bust we've had around here in the last decade."

Judge Hatfield's eyes narrowed. "What drug bust?" he asked.

"Junior Smitherton. He's been on my radar for a while, but after the storm hit, we seized a batch of pot plants out there at his trailer house. He was trying to disguise 'em as tomato plants and he almost got away with it. We got his ass locked up down in the jail."

"I always thought that boy was a doper," said Judge Hatfield. "Good work. But I still want y'all to be lookin' out for that head. I'm serious as a heart attack about that."

The sheriff sighed. "OK. I'll let the boys know and we'll do what we can."

16. Finius Works on WASTE

Finius was sitting at his desk stroking his gold-plated shoe-last. He had just placed a call to the deputy director of the procurement agency which was responsible for purchasing the products and services used by the federal government. In a town full of behemoth bureaucracies, the Washington Amalgamation for Services, Tools and Equipage (WASTE) was one of the biggest. But when it came to dealing with bureaucrats, nobody knew how to cut through red-tape faster than Finius. Nobody.

"Welcome to WASTE, how may I help you?" the deputy asked.

"Son, this is Congressman Finius Kochran, and I need to talk to you about a serious issue."

The deputy director perked up. He rarely got to talk to congressmen, but he knew all about Finius Kochran. "Of course, sir. What's the issue?"

Finius launched into his spiel. "My office is over here at the Cannon Office Building. This sonofabitch has 400 offices and most of 'em are multi-room suites with full baths. We also got conference

73

rooms with restrooms and we got a passel of public restrooms on every floor. Now I can't speak for everybody over here, but me and my staff are gettin' fed up with these nasty-ass bars of soap that y'all have been using in these lavatories."

"I see," the deputy director replied.

"I mean, this ain't a military barracks. We got all sorts of potentates that visit this place and I think it's high time that we step it up a notch."

"Do you prefer a different brand of soap?"

"No, son. I prefer a different *type* of soap. See, I've been listening to everybody's complaints and I've looked into things and most everyone agrees that we need to switch over to liquid soap. There's lots of new types of liquid soap being produced right now and it comes in all kinds of scents and flavors. What we can do is outfit the restrooms with plastic soap dispensers, and then you buy the liquid soap in bulk so the janitors can refill 'em whenever they run low. The soap is better. It smells better. It cleans better. And you ain't got a bunch of soap scum staining up the sinks like you do from them used-up bars of solid soap. It's more hygienic is what I'm saying."

"Is there much of a price difference?" the deputy asked.

"Well, frankly, I ain't really studied y'all's budget all that close, so I can't tell you for sure. But that ain't the only factor when it comes to takin' care of my staff and my guests and my constituents." Finius set his gold-plated shoe-last on his desk and gave it a twirl. "I guess I can take a look at the budgetary situation, but I reckon that one thing I'd find is that we probably ain't paying you and your colleagues enough for all your hard work. Let's see if we can get this soap business cured and then I'll see if it's not time to get some of you boys some well-deserved pay raises."

Now smiling from ear to ear, the deputy director leaned back in his worn-out office chair and said simply, "I'll look into it Congressman. I promise."

Finius thanked him, hung up the telephone, and grabbed his spinning shoe-last. *This is too easy*, he thought.

Day Four

17. The Consortium and the Latest News

Wednesday, March 10, 1982

5:30 a.m.

Paraclifta Hardware

Paraclifta, Arkansas

John D. Dalyrmple had never married and he lived alone in the home where he was born. He was a thoughtful man, but he had no idea why he was so incredibly superstitious. Some of his superstitions were grounded in science, like his refusal to drink milk while eating catfish. Others were simply strange.

There was a full moon on March 9, 1982. On the morning after a full moon, it was John D.'s custom to walk backward until 6:00 a.m. If anyone had ever asked him why, his only explanation would have been that it was bad luck not to do so. Therefore, he backed away from his bed when he woke up at 5:30 a.m. on Wednesday morning. Then he walked backward into the bathroom to shave and brush his teeth. After that, he walked backward to his dresser, slipped on some jeans and a fresh pocket tee shirt, and then backed his way out of his shotgun shack until he bumped into his pickup truck. Then he drove to the hardware store.

At 6:00 a.m., after he was freed from the obligation to walk backward, he hopped out of his pickup, selected one of the dozens

of keys hanging from his belt loop, and unlocked the back door of
the hardware store. He clicked on the coffee machine, fired up a
cigarette, and said hello to his compatriots as they filed into the
Consortium's chamber.

"Was you able to get much done yesterday?" he asked Buddy
Wayne.

"Yeah. We fixed a bunch of windows and helped out with a
couple of roofs," answered Buddy Wayne. "Dicey was able to help
me out yesterday morning."

"Well, I've got some news," announced Weaver. "The sheriff
called me yesterday and they arrested Junior. Turns out them plants
was dope plants."

"What do you mean dope plants?" asked Evelray.

"You know, Mary Jane. Grass. Whacky weed. Marijuana,"
answered Weaver. "The boy was makin' himself some left-handed
cigarettes."

"Did I, or did I not, say that that boy was a doper?" Buddy
Wayne said proudly.

"You did," Weaver agreed.

"No matter how you slice it, that's a real shame," said John D.

"Drugs … I just can't believe that people would do that to their
bodies," mused Frogeye amidst the milk-colored cigarette smoke
oozing out of his nostrils. "Folks really oughta take better care of
themselves."

Evelray leaned forward so he could look at all of his colleagues.
He lit a cigarette and said, "The drug problem is simple. The
Russians are tryin' to get people hooked on drugs, so it'll hurt our
productivity and make us docile."

On the other side of the table, Weaver exhaled his own stream
of smoke and announced, "Anyway, the sheriff was real thankful
that I figured it out. He even asked me if I ever thought about
being a deputy for 'em."

Frogeye pouted. "They ain't never asked me to be no deputy," he said.

"They ought to," said Evelray. "I bet you could help 'em crack lots of cases. You could locate all kinds of clues with them thick-ass glasses of yours."

The other men laughed while Frogeye continued to pout.

"Sheriff says Junior is lookin' at 40 years in jail," Weaver said.

"Damn," said Frogeye.

"Forty years in jail. Can you imagine that?" Buddy Wayne did some quick math in his head and said, "He'd be locked up 'til 2022. Damn."

"Might work out for the best, though," pondered Frogeye. "I reckon that humankind will have everything figured out by 2022. They'll probably be vaccinated against every kind of disease and they'll be flying around to other planets."

"Well I got some news too," added Evelray. "In addition to everything else that got tore up by that storm, the statue at the courthouse got its head blowed off. And guess who discovered it? The Chinquapin Lady."

"So what," said Buddy Wayne. "We got two stores ruined and gobs a people who still need repairs before the next rain. A statue head ain't no emergency."

Frogeye agreed. "Like I just said, 40 years from now, people won't be sittin' around worryin' about anything as silly as a statue."

"Well, I think it's a piss-poor reflection on our community if we don't get it fixed," Evelray countered. "If we was in Moscow and a statue of Joseph Leningrad got damaged, I betcha they'd get that fixed before they started working on anything else. Them communists don't mess around with stuff like that."

"I think them communists got their hands full," said John D.

Evelray continued, "I'll tell y'all one thing. The smartest move they ever made was to invade Afghanistan. After they get done takin' over that whole country, they're gonna have a warm-water port and then they'll go conquer Persia…. Y'all just sit back and watch."

"I didn't realize that you knew so much about military tackits," Frogeye said.

"I think you mean tack-tiles," said Buddy Wayne.

"Whatever," said Evelray. "And I'll tell y'all somethin' else. While we're over here barely able to pay for gasoline, they're gonna get control over all the oil—which they don't even need—'cause they're experts at nuclear power. They got this nuclear factory named Churn Noble that makes enough electricity to light up half the continent. They're way ahead of us and we dang sure better keep an eye on 'em."

Buddy Wayne had heard enough. "Well, y'all can stop discussin' military tack-tiles. What I mean is that I ain't sayin' they ought not fix that statue. I'm just sayin' it ain't that big a deal at the moment."

"What happened to his head anyway?" asked John D.

"Not sure, but it's long gone," answered Evelray.

John D. said, "That statue's been standin' there my whole life, but I don't reckon I've ever really looked at it."

"Me neither," said Weaver.

Frogeye turned and pointed at John D. "Hey, John D., if you got shipwrecked on an island and you could only have one thing, what would it be?"

Weaver raised his hand. "For me it'd be a .22 rifle," he said.

"OK, but you can only have one thing, which means that you wouldn't have no bullets," Frogeye replied.

"Oh."

The men pondered that subject for another fifteen minutes before they reached a consensus that the correct answer was *a woman*. Then John D. shooed off his colleagues so he could get the store open for business.

18. Judge Hatfield Calls His Paw-Paw

9:30 a.m.
Office of Judge Winthrop Hatfield
Paraclifta, Arkansas

Winthrop Hatfield had been raised by his great-grandfather, Jefferson Davis "J.D." Hatfield. J.D.'s only son and grandson had been killed in World War I and Word War II, respectively, so J.D. had assumed the role of serving as Winthrop's father.

At 107 years of age, J.D. was the oldest person in Paraclifta, and one of the oldest in the entire state. Despite his age, his mind was still as sharp as a tack and Winthrop frequently consulted him for political advice. Winthrop did not know much about J.D's father, except that he was a veteran of the Civil War. Nevertheless, Winthrop knew that J.D. would have sage advice about the Confederate war memorial, so he had decided to call his Paw-Paw to ask for help.

J.D. was still living independently, but was moving slow and closing in on deafness. For those reasons, Winthrop had to let the phone ring for several minutes before J.D. finally answered.

"Hello," said J.D.

"Hey, Paw-Paw, I need to ask your advice."

"OK."

"We got a problem at the courthouse."

"Is it all them tree limbs? Just get some inmates out there to clean it up. Them trees are gonna be fine."

"No," said Winthrop, "it's the Rebel statue."

J.D. perked up. "What the hell is wrong with it?"

"Well, the head done blew off of it during that storm," Winthrop explained.

The telephone line was quiet. After a minute of silence Winthrop tried again, "Did you hear me, Paw-Paw?"

"Yeah," he said. "I heard you. That just kinda' tears me up a little. I ain't never told you this, but the man on that statue is actually your great-great-grand-dad, Nahem Hatfield.... He was the last of the PIMPS."

"You're kidding," said Winthrop. "I never knew that."

"True story. He's the only one that made it back home. He was the youngest of the PIMPs, but he survived, and actually made it all the way up to Medium-Captain by the time the war ended. He never would talk about it. All he'd ever really say was *PIMPin ain't easy*. God only knows what all he musta' went through."

"Good Lord," said Winthrop. "How did he end up on the statue?"

"Well, it's kind of a long story. I was county judge when they decided to build somethin' and they wanted to honor the PIMPs. So I described daddy to the sculptor people and that's how they come up with the soldier. The Daughters of the Confederacy ladies wrote up the plaque, but since I was judge I didn't want it to look like I was using daddy for the statue and so I never told 'em and they didn't put no names on it.... But I can tell you, that man on that statue looks just like daddy."

"Wow," said Winthrop, "I wish I'd a known."

"Well, I reckon I shoulda told ya, but anyhow, you need to get that damn head fixed."

"Don't worry, Paw-Paw," Winthrop said, "I'm gonna fix it."

19. Sheriff Dingler Closes the Case

10:00 a.m.
Paraclifta Sheriff's Office
Paraclifta, Arkansas

Sheriff Dingler despised paperwork, but thanks to a federal grant secured by Congressman Finius Kochran, his department had recently purchased a copy machine. Today, Arlen was excited about the opportunity to finally put the machine to use. He was about to take a statement from Junior Smitherton and he needed a confession.

Junior was a 25-year-old high-school dropout who had never held down a job. Arlen had no reasonable doubt that the boy had been growing dope. Junior could not deny that he had been living in the mobile home where the pot plants were discovered. He had been caught *in flagrante delicto*. But if he denied ownership of the plants, it could make things difficult at trial.

In hindsight, Arlen realized that he should have had a deputy set up a watch on Junior and the plants. It would have been helpful to have a photograph of Junior watering them, or better yet, smoking them. He suspected he could send the fake tomatoes up to the crime lab and see if they contained Junior's fingerprints, but that was expensive and Judge Hatfield was always griping about the sheriff's office budget. *No*, he concluded, *what I really need is a clean confession.* And, thanks to the new copy machine, he had a plan.

The rectangular copy machine was two feet tall and three feet wide. It looked like a white plastic coffin that had been cut in half. Each of the ends had two plastic trays for different-sized paper and a control panel with blinking lights on the top edge. The top of the machine had a glass surface covered by a hinged lid. If you placed a document on the glass to make a copy, you would close the lid on top of the document to contain the flash while the machine took a photograph. The sheriff was about to use this newfangled machine to try to make Junior confess.

One of the deputies escorted Junior up from the jail in the basement of the courthouse. Arlen had decided to delay Junior's interrogation because he thought the boy looked a little *doped up* when he got arrested. If he did get a confession, he did not want to risk some clever defense lawyer arguing that Junior had started talking before he sobered up.

Arlen told the deputy to remove Junior's handcuffs and then he made his prisoner sit beside the big new copy machine.

"Son," Arlen said, "I'm fixin' to ask you some questions, and you need to tell me the truth. You're already in a heap of trouble, but if you start lying to me, it's gonna be even worse. Understand?"

Junior nodded his head.

"OK, now you ain't gotta talk at all, but if you don't, I'm gonna know you're guilty. And you can ask for a lawyer, but we ain't got no lawyers in this county, so we'll just have to hold you in the jail until we can get one up here. Do you understand them rights?"

Junior nodded again.

"Now if you tell the truth, we can get you out on bail 'til we figure out what to do about all this. But right now, I just need the truth out of you."

"OK," said Junior.

"Good." Arlen took Junior's hand and placed it on the top of the copy machine. Then he placed the lid down over the hand. "This here is a truth machine and it's 100% accurate. I need you to hold your hand very still and answer my questions. Ready?"

Junior fidgeted and began to sweat. "OK," he said.

"First, is your name Junior Smitherton?"

"Yes," said Junior.

The sheriff pushed one of the buttons on the control panel. The copy machine shook and rattled and then spit a sheet of paper into one of the trays. That paper reflected a photocopy of Junior's right hand, but the sheriff grabbed the top sheet from the *other* tray at the end of the machine. That sheet of paper contained this message:

TRUE STATEMENT

"Good," said Arlen as he showed the sheet to Junior. "Machine says that was true. Now, second question. Have you been staying at a trailer out on County Road 15?"

Junior's pulse had quickened and he rubbed his eyes with his left hand. *How can this machine know if I'm telling the truth,* he wondered.

"I need an answer, boy!" the sheriff barked.

"Yeah, that's true."

Once again the sheriff mashed a button and the copy machine rumbled and produced a sheet of paper. The sheriff retrieved a different sheet from a different tray and held it up where Junior could see it. It read:

TRUE STATEMENT

"Good. Now son, ain't it true that you was out there growin' your own dope plants?"

Junior had never been so nervous in his entire life. His brain was telling him that it was impossible for this machine to know anything about him or his truthfulness. The main thing he knew was that he did not want to spend 40 years in prison over some stupid plants. Finally, he looked at the sheriff and said, "No sir. That ain't true. I don't know nothin' about them plants."

Arlen stared into Junior's eyes and then he dramatically mashed the copy button on the machine. The machine vibrated and whirred. For Junior, it felt like time was standing still. *What's this damn machine gonna say,* he wondered.

Another sheet dramatically dropped into the bottom tray. As it did, the sheriff slowly slid the next sheet out of the top tray and looked at it quietly. Then he slammed it down on the table so that Junior could see its message. This time the note on the paper declared:

FLAT-OUT LIE!

Junior burst into tears when he saw the words on the paper. He pulled his right hand from the lie-detector machine and began rubbing his eyes.

"I'm really sorry, sheriff," he sobbed. "I wasn't hurtin' nobody and I wasn't gonna sell none of it. I use that stuff for medicine purposes."

"That's ok, son," said the sheriff. "You ought not have lied to me, but I appreciate you being honest now. I need to know how long you been growin' that stuff and if anybody else's been helpin' you."

"I'll tell you everything," Junior sniffled. "Just don't plug me back up to that truth machine."

Junior commenced to explain his entire criminal scheme. He insisted that all the plants were for his own personal use. Arlen concluded the interrogation and had the confession typed up for Junior to sign. Then, true to his word, he let Junior make bail and told him when he needed to be back for his trial.

20. What the Head Is Going On?

Paraclifta had a grand total of two restaurants. The Westside Diner and the East End Eat faced each other on opposite sides of Main Street. Unbeknownst to their customers, both cafés were owned by the same man, who lived in Little Rock. After opening the first restaurant in town, the man quickly realized that the town could support two eating establishments. Rather than face any competition, he decided to open a second café and completely corner the market. He hired separate employees for each store and made sure they operated independently. This prevented anyone from finding out about the common ownership while allowing the mysterious proprietor to secretly maintain a long-time monopoly over the Paraclifta restaurant industry.

Nobody in town patronized both businesses. Nobody. Instead, every resident would simply pick one or the other and then maintain that loyalty forevermore. At some point in life, each Paraclifta native had to make a crucial choice about where to dine. For folks in town, that choice was just as important as the other major life decisions they faced, such as deciding whether to smoke

89

cigarettes or to chew tobacco, or whether to deer hunt with a rifle or with a shotgun.

Many moons ago, Frogeye had chosen to do business with the Westside Diner. He could not remember why he made that decision, but he had never regretted it.

It was lunchtime, and the diner was busier than usual when Frogeye took a seat at one of the booths. As soon as he sat down, a perky waitress named Molly sashayed over to take his order. She had a long blond ponytail and her big red lips were smacking on a glob of chewing gum. She did not waste any time presenting Frogeye with a menu because she knew he would not need one.

"Hi, Frogeye. Whatcha need?" she asked.

"Hi, Molly. I reckon I'll take a glass of iced tea, fried bologna sandwich and some tater chips."

"Done," she said, "and how's it going?"

"Can't complain," he said. "Wouldn't do no good if I did."

"I heard that," she said, as she sashayed back to the kitchen.

Frogeye was watching her bottom as she walked away when he noticed a sheet of poster board hanging on the back wall. Someone had used a magic marker to make a sign that read:

NO HEAD

That's weird, he thought as he lit a cigarette. He was glad that Molly was back at work. She had stopped working for about a year after she finally had a child. She told Frogeye she had planned on staying home until she realized how hard it was to take care of a baby. Fortunately, she was able to return to work after her mom expressed a willingness to babysit during the day.

She was back in a flash to hand Frogeye his glass of iced tea.

"What's the deal with that sign?" he asked as he pointed to the poster board.

"Oh yeah," she said, "we just put that up this morning. Have you heard about the war monument at the courthouse?"

"Yeah. The head got blowed off."

"Exactly," said Molly. "Well, those morons over at the East End Eat put up a sign in favor of a new head for that statue. Word is, they got a jar by their cash register and they're taking up donations to help try to buy a new head."

"What's wrong with that?" asked Frogeye.

Molly dramatically stopped smacking her gum. She frowned and stared through Frogeye's thick glasses until she was looking directly into his frog eyes. Then she took a deep breath and said, "Well, a couple of things. First of all, that statue is a hundred years old and if the head popped off, maybe that's how God wanted it. Who really cares? Also, the government needs to do the fixin' if anything's needed. How do we know the East End's not just tryin' to scam people out of their loose change? And furthermore, it ain't none of their concern anyway. And finally, even if it wasn't for all them reasons, if they're for it, then we're gonna be against it over here. The East. End. Eat. needs to mind their own business."

Frogeye leaned away from Molly's stare and took a drag on his cigarette. Since he could not think of anything to say, he said simply, "I heard that."

"Good," she said as she flipped a straw onto the table and sashayed back to the kitchen.

I really think that statue needs a head, he thought as he waited on his bologna sandwich and tater chips

21. The Congressman Tours the Damage.

Finius Kochran loved publicity. It was tough to get noticed when you represented a rural district in the middle of nowhere, but he had made a name for himself in Washington by bullying his opponents and calling them communists when they opposed him or his interests. He was not an intelligent man, but he was a savvy political strategist. He was one of the very first politicians to realize the easiest way to keep the voters from being mad at him, was to make sure they stayed mad at each other. He did that by labeling his opponents as communists. This was a good way to deter disagreement because nobody wanted to be called a communist. Nobody.

He dreamed about the creation of a friendly television network that would blindly amplify his views and publicly chastise the communists who dared to disagree with him. But the journalists in his day were too smart for that. They provided impartial reports about his official activities and used facts to expose the instances when he lied in public. In short, the media were all a bunch of communists.

He never wanted anyone in his district to get hurt, but he appreciated a good tornado because he knew how to turn that into instant good publicity. Visiting a disaster site was like picking low-hanging fruit. It did not require him to read, research or prepare a speech. All he had to do was slip on one of his expensive suits and let the media watch him console a few victims. It was leadership, and he was a leader. It was also unlikely that any of those communist reporters would try to ambush him with legitimate questions about policy issues or his voting record. Visiting a disaster was easy, and nobody did it better than Finius. Nobody.

As a veteran politician, he knew to wait a few days after a disaster before making his visit. Otherwise, his detractors would say that he was impairing progress or just getting in the way. He also knew it took a couple of days to clear out all the dangers, like downed power lines. The last thing he wanted to do was get himself hurt, or mess up one of his good suits. Finally, he needed a couple of days to let the press know his plans so they could all be in the right place at the right time to get it all photographed and videoed. What good would it do to go out among the voters if nobody was there to report on it? For all of those reasons, he knew that the early afternoon, on the third day after the storm, was the perfect time for his grand appearance.

He was wearing one of his nicest suits when he arrived in Paraclifta. As usual, his necktie was hanging well below his beltline. Nobody was sure why he always wore his ties too long. One of his aides had suggested he would look more authentic if he put on a hat before he met with the locals, so he was also wearing a bright red baseball cap that had lettering across the top that read: *I'm a HARMer.* HARM stood for the Headquarters for Arms, Rifles and Muskets and it was a gun lobbying group that was one of his biggest supporters. He was always happy to help HARM.

Right after lunch, he met Judge Hatfield and Sheriff Dingler at the courthouse. Normally the local state representative would have participated in the tour, but Finius had told Judge Hatfield that he was not interested in sharing the limelight with Cammack Caflin. "Besides that," Finius had told Winthrop, "that boy ain't never introduced a bill and he's as worthless as tits on a billy goat."

Winthrop told Finius that the television crews had set up near the destroyed pharmacy building. He explained that he had arranged for the pharmacist and the owner of the service station to be on site so that the cameras could broadcast them visiting with their congressman.

When Winthrop had finished his briefing, the men began walking down Main Street toward the row of television cameras "Are you gonna be able to help with our statue?" Winthrop asked.

Finius stopped walking and turned toward Winthrop. "Well, I'm not sure. My aides tell me that it's not clear if we can use federal money on a Confederate statue, but I'm still working on it."

"Thanks," Winthrop said.

As the men resumed their walk, Finius turned to Winthrop again and said, "Let me do all the talking."

When they were a block away, Finius could see that the television cameras were already filming. There was white, gritty dust in the air and it caused Finius to cough. "What the hell is this shit?" he asked.

"It's probably just a little asbestos from the roof and insulation," replied Sheriff Dingler. "It won't hurt nothing, but I can get you a mask if you need one."

Finius was offended. "What kind of dumbass would wear a mask?" he asked. The only reason Finius had even come to town was so he could get on television. He was not about to cover up his face. Furthermore, he was worried that a mask might smear the makeup he wore when he was doing television work.

Soon the men were standing in a parking lot directly in front of the pile of rubble where the drugstore once stood. An adjacent lot held the remains of the service station. Its walls were intact, but the building looked like it had been stomped on by a giant. The two business owners emerged from a crowd of onlookers and walked up to Finius' entourage, where Winthrop made introductions.

The pharmacist looked like he belonged in a laboratory. He was wearing an ironed, button-up shirt with a white lab coat. The coat made him look extremely smart. The gas station owner looked like he belonged in a garage. He was wearing a greasy blue jumpsuit with a red bandana peeking out of one of the back pockets. The jumpsuit made him look like a hard-working man. He had on a black ball cap and his face was leathery and worn. He had dirt under all his fingernails and was wearing leather, steel-toed work boots, because that's what men wore.

Finius formed a look of concern and stepped toward the two men. He made sure to speak loudly, for the benefit of the reporters. "I'm going to make sure that the federal government helps you," he said. You will re-build, *blah, blah, blah*," he said.

"Thank you, Congressmen," said the business owners.

"My pleasure. You just let me know if you need anything," he said.

Then he faced the television cameras, removed his HARM hat and wiped his brow. The long bangs of his orange hair seemed to be oscillating beneath the asbestos grit drifting across the parking lot. "My office is committed to helping this community rebuild. We are all thankful that nobody was hurt. Nobody. These are the kind of hard-working people that the government is here to help and I can *promise* you that this town will build back and be stronger than it was before this tragedy, *blah blah blah*."

Winthrop and Arlen solemnly nodded their heads as Finius pointed to them. "I will work with these local leaders until the folks in Paraclifta are made whole. Thank you all for being here."

Finius's orange hair continued to waft in the breeze, like fairy floss on a stick of cotton candy. "Any questions?" he asked.

One of the television reporters stepped forward. "Congressman, there are reports that this town's Confederate statue was damaged by the storm, and there is some opposition to rebuilding it. In fact, there are some people who are arguing that it should not be located on public property in the first place and that it should be removed altogether. Can you comment on that?" she asked, as she pointed at him with her microphone.

Finius's face turned as red as the HARM hat he was holding in his hand. "Ma'am," he said, "that is simply fake news. This town has had a memorial statue for longer than I've been alive and if it needs to be fixed, then I don't see no reason why it can't be fixed. I don't know anything about people wanting to remove historical monuments, but I can only presume that anybody who wants to do that would be a communist."

Finius turned and strode back toward the courthouse with the Winthrop and Arlen in tow. As they walked away from the cameras, Finius noticed that the folks in the crowd were clapping.

"I guess the voters like what they heard," Finius said. "What the hell was that business about doing away with your statue?"

"No idea," said Judge Hatfield. "But we ain't removing that statue."

22. Cammack Comes to Town

Winthrop was looking out his office window at the busted catalpa trees when his secretary told him that State Representative Cammack Caflin was there to see him.

"Thanks D, send him in," said Winthrop.

Cammack stormed into Winthrop's office. He was furious about not being invited to Congressman Kochran's media blitz.

"Thanks a lot for telling me about the congressman's visit," he said sarcastically.

"I had nothing to do with any of that. He set everything up and was in complete control over it," Winthrop answered meekly. "I figured he'd let you know about it."

"Well, I thought y'all wanted my help. I guess I was wrong."

"Of course we want your help. We need all the help we can get."

Cammack was pouting. "It don't sound like it to me."

"Listen," Winthrop pleaded, "we've got some real problems. Top on the list is that our Rebel soldier statue got his head chopped off by the tornado. The one thing I needed out of Finius was some help with that, but he don't think the feds can do nothin' 'cause it's a

97

Confederate monument on state property. Now, people are all tore up about it and I can't figure out how to handle it. But we need a new head. Pronto. If you can get that fixed for us, you'll look like a genius and you'll poke Finius in the eye at the same time."

Cammack rubbed his chin and said, "I'd love to help with that. I bet I can get y'all some money to fix it and write up a law about it at the same time. Just to make shore this don't happen to nobody else in the state."

"Nobody," agreed Winthrop.

"Well, I reckon that if I'm gonna draw up a law, I'm gonna need to head up to Little Rock. I better head up there right now and get started on it," Cammack concluded.

"Sounds good," said Winthrop. "The sooner, the better."

23. The Media Ruin Everything

2:00 p.m.
OPPOSER Headquarters
St. Louis, Missouri

A few minutes after Finius snarled at the reporter who asked about the Paraclifta statue, video of the confrontation was broadcast on several local television stations. Rather than reporting on the plight of those who had suffered tornado damage and the plans to rebuild, the television stations opted to focus on the statue squabble. Tornados are newsworthy for a day or two, but nothing attracts viewers like a spirited, local imbroglio.

Shortly after the stories were aired, news of the controversy reached the headquarters of the Organization Promoting Protection of Significant Equal Rights (OPPOSER). Located in San Francisco, OPPOSER was a non-profit corporation which advocated for civil liberties. The group was not shy about filing lawsuits or organizing rallies whenever it took on a new cause.

OPPOSER's leader was a dashing, handsome attorney named Quincy Andrew Nguyen. Quincy, who was called Q-AN by his friends, was an infant when his Vietnamese parents emigrated to America. He had been home-schooled by his parents and had graduated first in his class. He had done so well that his parents

99

also awarded him a bachelor's degree (in Math), a master's degree (in History) and eventually a law degree. He was 30 years old by the time he completed his education and moved away from home.

He had a lot of work to do after missing out on the normal experiences of high school and college, so after opening his own law practice, he spent a great deal of time at night clubs and discos and soon became a ladies' man. He had risen to fame in the early 1970's when he defended a gentlemen's club in south Alabama. The club, which was named *Tits & Giggles*, had been charged with a misdemeanor after undercover police officers, posing as customers, observed performances by topless dancers. The officers used sophisticated cameras and video equipment and spent three months gathering evidence of the naked dancing. The evidence was eventually presented to the local district attorney who studied it for another two months before deciding to indict the club for one count of indecent exposure.

Q-AN attacked the state's case on two fronts. First, he argued that the club was protected by the First Amendment because the dancers were merely exercising their freedom of expression. In the alternative, he challenged the state's statute because the indecent exposure law prohibited only the public exhibition of *sexual organs*. Q-AN astutely argued that, as a matter of physiology, female breasts should not be classified as *organs*. He was able to proffer ample testimony to support his argument because there were plenty of college professors and medical professionals who were willing to give their opinions after they had reviewed the state's videos and photographs.

The case, *State of Alabama v. Tits & Giggles*, bounced around for several years until it finally ended up in the United States Court of Appeals for the Eleventh Judicial Circuit, in Atlanta, Georgia. While federal appellate courts usually designate a three-judge panel to rule on appeals, the Eleventh Circuit made a rare decision to have the case heard *en banc*, so that *all* of the judges could participate. The learned judges requested two sets of oral arguments, which was unprecedented at the time. Then they meticulously studied the state's evidence for an entire nine-month judicial term before dismissing the case.

After the ruling, the judges, along with Q-AN and the other lawyers, fully expected that the U.S. Supreme Court would take a look at *Tits & Giggles*. But when the Supreme Court declined, the Eleventh Circuit's ruling became final and the club was exonerated. Q-AN used *Tits & Giggles* to hone his legal skills, and by the time the case had concluded, he had emerged as a fierce advocate and one of the most famous lawyers in America.

He enjoyed fighting for the ideals of personal freedoms, but he enjoyed his fame even more. He loved to see his face on television and his name in the newspapers. After assuming command of the OPPOSERs, he was always on the lookout for high-profile cases that were suitable for his advocacy. He was excited to learn about the controversy surrounding the Paraclifta Confederate statue and he quickly summoned his chief legal aide to discuss it.

"Tell me what you know about this business with the Civil War monument," he said.

"All we know right now is that it's a Rebel soldier statue located at a county courthouse in Arkansas. The soldier's head got knocked off and now some people want the whole thing torn down, but nobody really knows what to do. Nobody," the aide said.

"What's our angle?"

"Well," the aide replied, "that's kinda' the problem. On the one hand, you could argue that the statue is offensive because it's a Confederate soldier. On the other hand, you could argue that it's merely historical. Even if it offends somebody, the First Amendment would probably still protect it. I don't think we can make any sort of religious challenge and we're not even sure who paid for it in the first place. I think we could make arguments for it *and* against it."

Q-AN rubbed his forehead. "Which position would generate the most news coverage?" he asked.

"Since it's in the South, I'm sure that most people down there would oppose it being removed."

"So, you're saying we should argue for its removal?" Q-AN asked.

"Personally, I think it's a local issue and we should stay out of it."

Q-AN began doodling on a sheet of typing paper. He liked to doodle while he was thinking. He looked up at his aide and asked, "Has anybody else taken a position on it so far?"

"Actually, the main reason that it's in the news is because Congressman Finius Kochran just yelled at a reporter over it," the aide answered. "He wants the statue left alone."

"Is that right?" asked Q-AN. "I cannot stand that pumpkin-headed fool. That settles it. The OPPOSERs need to get right in the middle of this. Have somebody make arrangements to get me down there tomorrow and be sure to alert the media."

24. Others Plan a Foray to Paraclifta

OPPOSER was not the only group taking an interest in the Paraclifta statue. The American Anglican Appreciation Association (AAAA) was a shadowy, loosely-organized group of disgruntled, prejudiced people. Its members were located all over the place and they typically communicated by telephone. It was difficult for the members to have meetings in person, but at least once a year they did their best to convene a meeting somewhere fun like Las Vegas. In 1981, they had held a get-together at the Indianapolis 500.

The members referred to their group as the *Foray* since that sounded the same as 4A. Whenever they were able to hold a formal meeting, they would chant: *Hooray for Foray!* Since the letter A is the first letter of the alphabet, the members would also show their allegiance by making the number one sign with their index fingers. Sometimes at sporting events, it was hard to tell if people in the crowd were *Foray* members or if they were just fans who thought their team was *NUMBER ONE*, or perhaps both. The more dedicated members of *Foray* also wore face coverings like the surgical face masks worn by medical workers. Outsiders assumed that the members wore these masks to obscure their identities. Actually, the masks served as a symbol of *Foray's* opposition to immigrants who could potentially be bringing germs or spreading airborne diseases into the U.S.

Whenever the group was able to convene a meeting, it would end up being a small crowd of people in surgical masks who would thrust their index fingers into the air and chant, *hooray for Foray!* If the members had extra time and were gathering at a suitable location, they would occasionally make a number one out of sticks or trash and then set it afire. Mostly, everyone would simply sit around and visit while enjoying food (usually barbecue) and drinks (usually beer) and smoking cigarettes (usually unfiltered non-menthols). Of course, the members would have to remove their masks for those activities.

The members of *Foray* did not have any official corporate charter or bylaws, but they did share common agreement on a few principles. The members considered themselves to be activists. Their friends considered them to be weird. The Southern Poverty Law Center considered them to be a hate group.

There had been a few isolated occasions when the group had shown up somewhere for a demonstration after a sufficient number of members had been able to get away from work. So, when *Foray* found out that people might be trying to remove a Confederate statue in Paraclifta, they decided that this should be one of those isolated occasions. The group's leaders decided that they would send an advance team to Paraclifta to pass out some tracts and membership applications and then they would plan a big rally at the controversial statue on Saturday, when most of their members would have the day off.

The *Foray* secretary maintained a spiral notebook containing all of the members' names, addresses and phone numbers. It was his job to notify members whenever the group planned a rally or get-together. Since they were planning an event in Arkansas, the secretary concluded that he should start with the members from that state. He flipped through the notebook until he found the first name with an Arkansas address. The member's name was Cammack Caflin.

Day Five

25. Weaver and His List of Firsts

Thursday, March 11, 1982
5:00 a.m.
Home of Weaver Gillham
Paraclifta, Arkansas

W eaver woke up extra early and eased outside to wander around his gargantuan garden. He was cautious about snakes. For years he had maintained a journal, which he called the *first list*, wherein he recorded natural beginnings and seasonal precedents. He recorded the date for events like the first bean sprout, the first tomato bloom and the first okra pod. In addition to vegetable breakthroughs, the list reflected other natural milestones, such as the first mosquito, the first firefly and the first snake. This year's list already had an entry for the first snake. It was the earliest snake-sighting he had ever recorded. He had no idea why the snakes were already out.

Weaver had always loved spring time, when the hardwoods' leaves would return to offer shade against the approaching torridity of long summer days. He loved the dogwoods and daffodils and he cherished sowing his crops. His only complaints about the spring were the terrible thunderstorms and terrifying twisters that inevitably tore through the countryside in advance of the doldrums of summer. He looked at the sky as the first light of day began to stretch over the horizon. *It ain't gonna rain today,* he concluded.

As he was walking back to his house, he saw dozens of spider webs in the field beyond his vegetable patch. He paused to stare at the stunning display. The splendid webs, sprinkled with dew, appeared to be glowing in the morning light. They were all the same size and shared the same, precise design. It reminded him of his days in basic training where the Army base had row after row of identical barracks. The barracks, like these webs, were exact replicas of one another.

Those barracks had been designed by engineers, aided by measurements, maps, surveys and rigid blueprints. *How did these spiders manage to be so precise,* he wondered. *Did they have a meeting where older spiders provided web-making training? Would they get angry if one of their friends developed a different web design? Probably not. And, they would never waste time building a stupid statue.* The spiders crafted identical webs because nature dictated it. He loved the natural order of the universe. It was why he knew there was a God.

He also knew it would be weeks before he picked his first ripened tomato. *What was Junior thinking when he tried to disguise his marijuana plants? Didn't he understand nature?* As he was meditating about nature, he heard a mockingbird cycling through her calls. He loved mockingbirds and he hoped this one would nest near his garden. *First mockingbird of the year,* he thought. *I've got to write this on my first list.*

26. The Consortium Grows Concerned

Since the moon was now waning, John D. was running ahead of schedule because he was no longer required to spend the early morning walking backward. Since his commute was running ahead of schedule, he decided to make a couple of passes on Main Street to review the progress of the cleanup.

Driving through town so early allowed him to look at the homes around town and see who was already awake. As he suspected, the answer was everybody. He knew that everyone under the age of 60 was either in school or had a job. *Except for Junior Smitherton,* he thought. Hardworking people had to get up before daylight. Not only that, he knew that he and his neighbors were accustomed to going to bed early. Every local business was closed by 6:00 p.m. and the people in town could only pick up three television stations, if they were lucky. Unless you had to go to out of town for a high school football game, there was simply no reason to stay up late.

As he looked around town, he could tell that a large amount of debris had been loaded up and hauled away and he was not surprised to see men on backhoes were already at work amongst the rubble. But he realized that something was out of place when he drove by the cafes. Each of them had a poster board sign in the plate glass window next to their front doors. He stopped in the street and saw that the sign at the East End Eat read:

NEW HEAD

Across the street, a sign at the Westside Diner announced:

NO HEAD

He wondered about those signs as he continued driving to the alley that ran behind the hardware store. He remembered Evelray talking about the missing head on the courthouse statue. *But why would the diners care about that?* he wondered.

He opened up the backdoor of the hardware store and was sitting by the cash register with a cigarette and a cup of coffee when the rest of his Consortium cohorts shuffled in.

After the men exchanged their greetings, Weaver asked, "Reckon deer ever get killed in a tornado?"

"I wouldn't thank so," answered Buddy Wayne. "They probably got sense enough to run for cover and hunker down."

As the other men were voicing their agreement, John D. interrupted them. "What's the deal with them signs at the diners about *no head* and *new head?*"

"It's a mess, is what it is," said Frogeye. "I was in the Westside yesterday and they're all worked up 'cause the East End people are raising money for a new head for that statue at the courthouse."

"Who cares about that?" asked John D.

"I'll tell you one person that cares and that's Congressman Kochran," Evelray announced. Evelray happened to be a big fan of the congressman. A couple of years ago, he had actually talked to the man on the telephone, twice in the same week. He had enjoyed the conversations but his monthly telephone bill had been so high he had vowed to never make another long-distance call. "He was down here yesterday and the fake news people tried to get him to say that we needed to get rid of our statue."

"Who are the fake news people?" asked Frogeye.

"Well, you know what I mean," Evelray responded. "Them news people are always tryin' to create a story so they can sell more advertising. They try to make everything overly sensual."

"I think you mean *sentimental*," offered Weaver.

"He means *sensational*, you dumbasses," Frogeye said. "And them media people ain't trying to make fake news. They just report on stuff. They're just regular folks like the rest of us." A couple of years ago, Frogeye had developed a crush on a television reporter from Little Rock. She had left the television racket, but he still thought about her, bye and bye.

John D. made a declaration. "Irregardless of that, I'm tryin' to figure out why the diners give a damn about the courthouse statue. That thing's been there forever and nobody's ever even paid no attention to it. Hell, when the damn head plopped off, nobody even noticed that for three days. Nobody."

Evelray was starting to get agitated. "Like I said yesterday, I think that statue is important. It's a part of our history and I *have* paid attention to it. It talks about the men from our town who fought in the war and it reminds everybody that soldierin' ain't easy."

"It actually says *pimpin ain't easy*," said Buddy Wayne. "I remember from lookin' at it when I was a kid and the school took us over there on a field trip."

"I didn't know you ever went to school," said Frogeye with a chuckle.

Evelray pointed at Buddy Wayne. "That right there proves my point. The school kids need stuff like that statue. It makes 'em 'preciate our lineage."

Now Buddy Wayne was agitated. He aimed the only remaining finger of his left hand back at Evelray. "Don't mean we need to waste tax dollars on fixin' the thing. I'm glad you looked at it once during the sixty-five years you've lived here, but I bet I could count on one hand the number of people who'd actually give a rat's ass if it got fixed or not. And I ain't got but a total of four and a half fingers."

John D. decided he needed to take control. "Fellas," he said calmly, "let's settle down. If the cafes want to fuss about it, that's one thing. But we're better than that."

The men seemed to calm down.

"You're probably right. I don't like this kind of contentment," said Weaver.

"I think you mean *contemptment*," offered Buddy Wayne.

"He means *contention*, you dumbasses," said Frogeye.

"Irregardless," said John D., "I reckon the Consortium should stay out of it. Let's let other people sort it out."

Buddy Wayne decided to change the subject. "I had Dicey helpin' me out again yesterday and we was patchin' a roof for this widow woman and she's got problems with her hot-water heater. I don't thank it's on account of the tornado, but it ain't workin' right. I looked at it and it's got an extra line what runs out the top."

"Are you talkin' about Worm's house?" asked Evelray.

"That's right. It was Worm's widow's place."

"I know exactly what you're talking about," said Evelray. "I put that tank in back in nineteen and seventy-one. I'll ease over there later this mornin' and get it fixed for her. How's she doin' anyway?"

Buddy Wayne: "She had a rough spell after Worm died, but she's a good ole gal. That storm scared the fool out of her."

Frogeye stubbed out his cigarette, looked at the ceiling and made an observation. "What I like about a small town is that you know everybody, which means you always know who you're dealing with. Not only that, you know peoples' vehicles. If I see somebody's pickup at the diner, and it's somebody I don't like, I can just drive on by. You ain't got that in big cities where ever body is a stranger."

"That's true," Buddy Wayne agreed. "Maybe people in big cities should wear name tags that let ya' know what kinda person they are. Like a tag that says, *I'm a jackass*, or *Don't believe me, I'm a liar.*"

John D. chuckled. "I reckon that'd be helpful."

"In the meantime, we're lucky that twister hit on a Sunday. It might of killed some folks if it'd rolled through downtown on a weekday afternoon," said Evelray.

"I heard that," said Frogeye. "But I got a question for John D. Do you still have seven years of bad luck if your mirror gets broke in a tornado?"

John D. replied, "It's only if *you* break a mirror. Not if you have a mirror that gets broke by an act of God. Don't be ridiculous, Frogeye."

"Oh."

"Well, anyway, I reckon I need to get opened up," John D. said. "See y'all tomorrow."

The Consortium was adjourned.

27. Offensive Handbills

Like all respectable citizens, the Chinquapin Lady started her day by reading the newspaper. When she walked outside to fetch her Thursday paper, she was surprised to find a pamphlet lying on top of it. It was some kind of brochure that looked like an ordinary sheet of typing paper, folded in half. The front and back of each section had a different message and the very back page contained an invitation to join an organization called the American Anglican Appreciation Association (AAAA).

At first, the Chinquapin Lady did not read any of the leaflet, but as she was wadding it up, she noticed that similar pamphlets were all over her neighborhood. Some had been stuck to mailboxes and placed under windshield wipers while others were simply lying on the sidewalk. *Who would make such a mess*, she wondered. She smoothed out the wadded paper and began to read its message. Then she looked at the sky and yelled, "I KNEW IT!"

28. Dorinda Takes Offense

Judge Hatfield got to the courthouse earlier than usual because he was obsessed about the headless statue which, he now knew, had been fashioned in the likeness of his own great-great grandfather, the former Paraclifta PIMP. *I'm gonna fix that head if it harelips the devil,* he thought. He had little doubt that he could order a replacement head, but he was worried about how about how long it would take. *Where do you buy marble for statues,* he wondered. He also had fiscal concerns. His first priority was to finish clearing out all the storm debris and help get the drugstore running again. Meanwhile, the sheriff's office was already low on funds and money did not grow on trees. And speaking of trees, the courthouse catalpas were still a mess.

He was also frustrated about the outside agitators and their contrived controversy about the Confederate cenotaph. He knew that the bickering would continue as long as there was a headless statue on the courthouse square, but he needed to find some money before he could pay someone to fashion a face. *Surely the state or the feds can at least help with some funding.*

He was deep in thought and pacing around his office when Dorinda let herself in.

She was holding one of the *Foray* pamphlets that someone had placed on her porch. She threw it at her boss and screeched, "What are you gonna do about this?"

Winthrop kept his back ramrod straight as he bent over to retrieve the handbill. He had never heard of *Foray*. Dorinda had her arms crossed and her body was swaying from side to side. She stared at her boss with a scowl on her face as she watched him start reading the pamphlet.

Winthrop glanced at his swaying secretary. "D, let me ask you something. Did you look at this?"

"No!," she shrieked. "I ain't gonna read that racist nonsense."

As Winthrop studied the pamphlet, he thought about the day four years ago when he had first hired Dorinda. He needed a new secretary and he had consulted his Paw-Paw for advice. "You should hire a minority" J.D. had told him. "Voters love that shit."

It was an easy choice for Winthrop because he had grown up with Dorinda's parents and he had known her his entire life. He believed that hiring her had been a fantastic decision. She was dependable, kind and helpful. She was also very attractive. Through the years, he had grown to consider her a personal friend.

He did not want her to be upset, but he believed he had worked with her long enough that he could have a little fun with her. He hiked up his sans-a-belt slacks and plopped into the chair behind his desk. He used the pamphlet to point to one of the chairs in front of his desk and told Dorinda to take a seat.

Without uncrossing her arms, Dorinda maintained her angry glare and sat down on the opposite side of the desk.

Winthrop looked back to the pamphlet, looked Dorinda straight in the eyes, and said, "Let me ask you a few questions and I need you to be honest."

"OK," she mumbled.

"Tell me if you agree with these things. First, the education system in America is failing."

"I think we could do a whole lot better in how we school our kids," she said. "I agree with that."

"OK," said Winthrop, "How about this, it is too hard for people to find good jobs in this country."

"You know that's right," she replied. "If you hadn't hired me back in '78, I'd probably be unemployed. I love this job, but lots a people ain't been as lucky as me and we do need more good jobs for folks."

Winthrop continued, "There is too much crime in America."

"Everybody knows that," she said. "I heard they just locked up Junior Smitherton for growing dope right here in our county. We dang sure need to do something 'bout all the crime in this nation."

Winthrop nodded and said, "There are too many immigrants crossing our borders, taking our jobs, depleting our resources and spreading germs and diseases."

Dorinda was quiet for a moment and then said, "I think that's probably right. My family has been here for four generations and we work and pay our taxes. I ain't real happy about foreigners that come over just 'cause they wanna take jobs away from our own folks. So I guess I agree with that."

"Got it," said Winthrop. "Now what about this one. Jews control our banking system and make it impossible for regular Americans to get affordable credit."

"Hmm," said Dorinda. "I don't know nothin' about who runs the banks, but I always heard that it's Jewish people. I ain't got no problem with Jewish folks. In fact I ain't never met one. But I can say this— it ain't easy gettin' a loan and the interest rates are shore too high."

"So you kind of agree with that one?" Winthrop asked.

"I agree that it's too hard to get a loan," she clarified.

"OK," Winthrop continued. "I've just got one more to run by you: All the Jews, Mexicans, Orientals and Blacks should be sent back to their home countries."

"Are ya outta yo' mind, Winthrop? That's the stupidest damn thing I ever heard!" Dorinda shriekd. "Hell no, I don't believe that."

"Well, I don't neither," Winthrop said. "But you might be interested to know that the group that gave you this flier has a list of six *Tenets of Truth*. And you just told me that you agree with five out of the six. It looks like you got more in common with 'em than you think."

"Winthrop, you're crazy," Dorinda said with a chuckle. "But them folks is still racist and I'm afraid they're tryin' to make trouble 'round here."

"Don't worry," Winthrop answered. "I ain't gonna allow no trouble."

Dorinda turned around and headed back to her desk and Winthrop wadded up the pamphlet and threw it in the trash. *I don't like this one bit*, he thought. *I've gotta get that head fixed and get rid of these damn carpetbaggers.*

29. Q-AN Comes to Town

Q-AN and four of his female staff members flew into the Little Rock airport around 7:30 a.m. and rented two cars for the drive to the boondocks. When he and his entourage arrived in Paraclifta, they decided to take a tour around town. The tour took three minutes. The only thing that looked interesting was the tornado rubble. Luckily there were plenty of news media gathered at the courthouse awaiting the press conference.

Q-AN dispatched one of his helpers to walk down Main Street to search for hotels and bars. He leapt out of his rental car, snatched up his favorite Louis Vuitton briefcase and confidently marched to the edge of the courthouse lawn, near the headless statue, to address the throng of reporters.

"Friends, my name is Quincy Andrew Nguyen and I am the Chairman of the Organization Promoting Protection of Significant Equal Rights. Whenever there is inequity, the OPPOSERs are there. Whenever there is inequality, the OPPOSERs are there. Whenever there is injustice, the OPPOSERs are there. Whenever something needs to be opposed, the OPPOSERs are there to oppose it."

He pointed at the Rebel statue. "Today we are here to oppose this statue. This statue has no place in America and it should be removed. It should be replaced with a monument that can be embraced by people of all races and nationalities, by all genders and by all religions and no religion. The Constitution requires that public monuments should inspire domestic tranquility and promote the general welfare of the people. They should be for the people, and by the people."

Suddenly Q-AN paused because he could not remember the name of the town where he was located. Then he continued, "I am proud to be here *in this town* and I am going to stay here and do whatever it takes to deal with this monument situation. If we have to protest, we will protest. If we have to file suit, we will file suit and if we have to appeal, then we shall appeal. But the OPPOSERs and I will not yield and will not depart." Then he shouted, "WE WILL NOT LEAVE THIS PLACE UNTIL JUSTICE IS DONE!"

For his rousing conclusion, he accidentally conflated the lyrics from the battle songs of the Union and Rebel soldiers. He lifted his arms and turned his face to the sky and said:

> Mine eyes have seen the glory,
> In Dixie Land, we'll take our stand.
> Glory, glory hallelujah.
> Look away, Look away, Dixie Land.
> His truth is marching on.

His presentation had been spellbinding. The media members were not exactly sure what sort of message he was trying to convey, but they all agreed that he had spoken with charisma and eloquence, and they were more than satisfied that it was newsworthy.

As the reporters began to work on their dispatches, Q-AN and his companions declined questions and slowly walked back to their rental cars where the aide he had sent to scout for accommodations was waiting for them.

"Did you find us a hotel?" he asked her.

"This town does not have any hotels," she replied.

Q-AN looked concerned. "Damnit," he said. "What about a place to grab a drink?"

"They tell me it's a dry county," she reported.

"What the hell is a dry county?"

"Apparently it's against the law to serve alcohol in this county."

"Do what?" said Q-AN.

"Most of the counties down here don't allow the sale of alcohol. The closest place that does is about a hundred miles away."

"Son of a bitch," said Q-AN. "That's a constitutional violation if I ever heard one."

"Sir," she asked, "what do you want to do?"

"I want to get the hell out of here," he replied. "Take me back to the airport."

And in short order, Q-AN and the OPPOSERs departed from Paraclifta.

30. Cammack Writes a Law

Arkansans were glad that their state legislature only met one time every other year. The people did not want much law and the General Assembly was not inclined to give them much.

When the General Assembly convened for its biennial sessions, the legislators gathered at the glorious State Capitol Building in Little Rock. The Capitol Building is a grand structure, capped with a monumental dome that makes it closely resemble its federal counterpart in Washington, D.C. The building was constructed in 1915 on the site of a state penitentiary, which was helpful, because all of the labor was supplied by prisoners. The building is surrounded by beautifully-landscaped gardens and spectacular monuments. Ironically, one of the monuments is a statue honoring Confederate women and it was designed by the same sculptor who created the Paraclifta PIMP.

The Capitol Building was very quiet in the spring of 1982 since the legislature was out of session. But it came to life on March 11, when State Representative Cammack Caflin held a press conference to discuss the first bill he had ever written. The press conference took place on the second floor of the building, just outside the Assembly Hall. At precisely 10:00 a.m., Cammack strolled up to a podium and looked out at a handful of reporters and television cameras. As he glanced at his notes, he realized that he was not very nervous. *Maybe this is where I belong,* he thought. *In front of the cameras.*

He cleared his throat and leaned into the microphones. "Ladies and Gentlemen, thank you for your attendance. My name is State Representative Cammack Caflin, and I represent a portion of South Arkansas that includes Paraloma and Paraclifta. Today I would like to talk to you about POOPIE."

Cammack paused for a moment and realized that the only sounds in the great hall were the whir of television cameras and the clicks of regular cameras.

He continued: "I know that you have heard about the statue controversy in Paraclifta. Well, my answer to that is—POOPIE. I have drafted a bill for the Protection of Official Plaques in Existence. This state needs protection from the federal government and from outside agitators, and POOPIE gives us that protection. POOPIE does several things. It protects our plaques and monuments. It lets state and local governments fix them monuments, like the one in Paraclifta that needs to be fixed. And, it also makes it illegal for the feds or anyone else to prevent us from fixin' any of them monuments that need fixin'."

Cammack had a strained look on his face and he was starting to sweat. He spoke slowly, with a strong southern drawl. "We've got to protect our historical monuments," he said. But, because of his accent, it sounded like he was asking for protection of *hysterical* monuments. Fortunately, the reporters understood what he meant because they all had similar accents.

Cammack pointed to a stack of papers on the table in front of the podium. "I wanna give y'all a copy of my new law. I wrote it myself 'cause we can't run the risk of any trouble if any more of our important plaques and monuments need to be fixed. We've got to protect our hysterical monuments, and that's no joke. I'm very proud of this new law."

He used his jacket sleeve to wipe the sweat from his face and then he looked at the reporters for his grand finale. "I have every confidence that my colleagues in the General Assembly will get behind me, and help me pass POOPIE."

When he finished his speech, he expected to hear a roar of applause, but then realized the only people listening to him were media members who had to stay neutral. He instantly knew he had made a mistake. *I should have brought a crowd of supporters to cheer for me*, he thought. *Oh well, at least I finally wrote a bill and now I'm finally gonna get noticed around here.* He looked out at the reporters and was delighted to see that they were all reading copies of his new bill.

AN ACT TO BE ENTITLED:
Protection Of Official Plaques In Existence.

Date: March 11, 1982
Sponsor: Honorable Cammack Caflin

Section 1: A historical monument is any statue, memorial, plaque, object or item or thing that honors or memorializes any historical or fictional person or likeness.

Section 2: The government shall not allow for the damage, destruction, defacement, defamation, disparagement or decapitation of any historical monument.

Section 3: If any historical monument is damaged, destroyed, defaced, defamed, disparaged or decapitated, then state or local government can fix it.

Section 4: Neither the federal government or anyone else can prevent a historical monument from being fixed.

Section 5: So help us God.

The reporters seemed to be very interested in Cammack's POOPIE. He had never been prouder. As he was basking in self-glory, one of the reporters raised her hand.

"Representative, this is Sally Sutterfield from the *Arkansas Journal*. Because of the conflict over the Rebel statue in your district, we understand that a group of racists has been passing out leaflets and is advertising a rally in Paraclifta on Saturday. A lot of people are upset about this and we'd like to know if you have any comment."

"Hmm," said Cammack, "I reckon that my new law will help with that situation, but you need to remember, there are very fine people on both sides of this issue."

"Are you saying that the people who are passing out racist literature in your district are *very fine people?*" asked the reporter.

"Sure," answered Cammack.

"OK," said the reporter. "I don't have any other questions."

Cammack felt great. He was about to get some publicity after all, just not the kind he was hoping for.

31. Finius Fires Back

Finius found out about Cammack's press conference less than five minutes after it had concluded, and it had made him hotter than a pepper sprout.

"I want my whole staff in here at once!" he yelled from his personal office.

Two secretaries, four of his aides, and two interns sprinted in and stood nervously in front of his desk. Finius grabbed his gold-plated shoe-last and banged it on his desk.

"That no-account communist Cammack Caflin thinks he's really clever. He's done written up a state law about monuments. POOPIE is what is. He's tryin' to get all the credit for takin' care of the Paraclifta PIMP statue. And worse than that, he's tryin' to make it where the feds can't be involved."

Finius stared across his desk and methodically looked into the eyes of each one of his staff members. After staring them down, he continued with his tirade. "Here's what I want, and I want it fast. I want my own bill that keeps the states from having anything to do with monuments and that makes it absolutely clear that if there's

DAY FIVE   129

gonna be any monument meddlin' or maneuvering, it'll be Congress that does it! Not some piss ant state legislature. I want the finished product to be a lot stronger than POOPIE. Understand?"

His staff members knew better than to ask any questions. "Yes, sir," they dutifully replied.

"Then skedaddle, and get it done before the day's over!" he barked.

As his staff members scurried out of his office he used his gold-plated shoe-last to whack his desk again. *This is bullshit,* he thought.

32. The Diners Dig In

While Finius's staff worked on a new law, tensions were rising in Paraclifta's two diners. Frogeye was walking up the sidewalk on Main Street when he noticed that the Westend Diner now had a large red banner hanging across the entire storefront which announced:

New Head = NO SERVICE

What in the world, he wondered, as he approached the café. Before he could make it to the front door, Dicey Davidson darted across Main Street and whipped out his tape measure. Frogeye stopped when he saw that Dicey was studying the new sign.

"You fixin' to measure that?" he asked.

"Yep," said Dicey.

"Need me to hold the tape for ya?"

"Yep," said Dicey.

Dicey handed him the end of the tape and then walked along the banner until he reached the other end. Dicey fumbled with his measuring machine and then put his face directly on his end of the tape. It looked like his nose was touching the stainless-steel case. "Sixty-four inches!" he yelled.

"I reckon that's pretty big," replied Frogeye.

Dicey wasn't finished. He motioned to Frogeye to let loose of his end of the tape. Frogeye did and the aluminum tape slithered back to the stainless-steel case that Dicey was still grasping. Once the tape had fully retracted, Dicey pulled it out again and measured the banner's width.

"Sixteen inches, and one-half, and three of them little notches!" he shouted. "That's how much it is up-and-down-wise."

"Good work," said Frogeye. "Have you ate lunch yet?"

"Nope," said Dicey. "I been checkin' measures."

"Well, let me buy ya a bologna sandwich and some chips," offered Frogeye.

Dicey clipped his tape measure back to his belt and followed Frogeye to a table in the middle of the diner. Molly the waitress was working again.

"Hey, boys," she said as she smacked on her glob of gum. "How'd ya' like our new sign?"

"It's sixty-four inches cross-wise, and not as much as that, up-and-down-wise," Dicey announced.

"Thanks, Dicey," said Molly. "We're proud of it. Maybe those morons over at the East End Eat will get the message."

Frogeye scrunched his eyes. He looked like a frog wearing a baseball hat and thick glasses. What in the Sam Hill is going on?" he asked.

"I told y'all that they was over there trying to raise money for a head. Well now they done got a bunch a people stirred up and we had some crazy lawyer come down here to try to get the whole statue tore down. And now we got some creepy racists goin' around and spreadin' hateful handouts. Everything's gettin' outta hand and it's all 'cause the East Enders stuck their nose where it don't belong."

Frogeye nodded. "You may be right, but how do you know that they wasn't just tryin' to legitimately raise money to fix the statue?"

"You know better 'n that, Frogeye. They was—and they still is—up to no good. If the statue needs to be fixed, then the county can, and will, do the fixin'. They ain't got no more business tryin' to ramrod gettin' a new statue head than they do tryin' to steal our chocolate gravy recipe, which is what we heard that they have done."

"I didn't know they was making chocolate gravy," said Frogeye.

"Well apparently, they started right after we did. But it ain't near as good as ours."

"Hmm," said Frogeye. "Dicey, reckon what you wanna eat?"

"Chocolate gravy," he said.

"Good choice," Molly said through her chewing gum. "I'll bring you a bowl of that and a basket of buttermilk biscuits."

"I thought it was lunchtime," Frogeye noted.

"We sell it all the live-long day," replied Molly.

"You learn somthin' new all the time," said Frogeye. "Bring me the same thing. And bring us both a glass of ice tea."

"Comin' up," Molly said as she sashayed back to the kitchen.

"That statue at the courthouse ain't got a head," said Dicey.

Frogeye nodded and said, "That's true, and it's turnt into a real problem."

The men were quiet for a minute and then Frogeye looked at Dicey and said, "Reckon you'd have time to help me haul some firewood out to my deer camp this evening?"

"Can I do some measurin'?"

"You shore can."

"OK, then."

The men got quiet again and waited on their biscuits and gravy.

33. Finius Lets Loose His Own Legislation

Finius was always too big for his britches. At least that what his mother used to tell him when he was a boastful boy. "Everybody has to salute somebody," she would say. "You can't always be the one in charge."

The problem was that Finius *wanted* to be the one in charge. He believed he deserved to be in charge. He sorely wanted to become a U.S. Senator and he fantasized about becoming President. He believed he was smart enough to be the chief executive, but he knew the odds were against him. Despite his mother's familiar quote, Finius had never saluted anyone and he knew that could be a political problem.

When he became eligible for the draft, he studied the list of medical conditions which could disqualify him from military service. Luckily he had one of them—a bone spur on his wrist. This was fortunate for someone who did not have the time or inclination to serve in the military. Finius had other priorities. He was able to avoid conscription after he convinced his doctor to write a letter confirming the bone spur. Being deemed ineligible for service was the happiest moment of his life, until he got elected to Congress. Now, he worried that he could never run for President because his opponents would label him a draft-dodger. *Nobody who avoided military service could ever be elected President,* he thought. *Nobody. Maybe people in the North could tolerate it, but people in the South would never get behind a man who avoided the Army.*

If not for his political ambitions, he would have never given his draft-avoidance a second thought, but now it was often heavy on his mind. Every year, his office received requests from high school seniors in his district who sought appointment to one of the military service academies. He always looked at the applications with a jaundiced eye, fearing that one of those kids would end up coming home to run against him some day. But he would always approve his allotment of nominees and write each one of them a fancy letter thanking them for volunteering to serve their country. *We are proud for your commitment, blah, blah, blah.*

Despite his concerns, he was sitting at his desk daydreaming about a presidential campaign. *Maybe people will understand that a bone spur is a serious health problem,* he told himself as he stroked his gold-plated shoe-last. *It's not my fault that they wouldn't let me enlist. If anybody calls me a draft-dodger, maybe I can just scream* fake news *and call them communists.* He looked at his wrists. It had been so long ago, he had forgotten which one had the lucky spur that had rescued him from the draft.

He tossed his shoe-last into the air and looked at one of the framed pictures on his office wall. Despite being married and having two sons and a grandson, the only pictures in his office depicted his favorite, tangible, possessions. He had a large framed photograph of his Washington residence, a smart townhouse on DuPont Circle. He also had a painting of the Colorado mansion where he spent most of the summer months, along with photographs of his Mercedes-Benz 380 and the sailboat he kept at Martha's Vineyard.

When he showed people around his office, he would brag on his possessions the way normal people would brag on their children. He would point to the Colorado house and say, "This is my pride and joy. He just turned 18 years old." When showing off the photograph of his boat, he would say, "This is my little girl, *Drifting and Drafting.* I like to sail when I'm drafting up new laws." Of course, he would also make sure to show visitors his gold-plated shoe-last.

As he continued tossing the shoe-last into the air, his thoughts wandered to his new legislation. He had given his staff a 4:00 p.m. deadline to have his new bill ready. He had learned that most of the national media were ready to enjoy happy hour at the end of the workday. That was fine with him because nobody loved happy hour more than Finius. Nobody. In order to make the evening news cycle *and* stay in good with the media, he had scheduled a 4:30 p.m. press conference to announce his new legislation.

All afternoon he had been fuming over Cammack's proposed state law. He knew that the Arkansas state legislature would not even be able to vote on *anything* until the session convened next year. Cammack's proposal was probably just a publicity stunt, but it had gotten him on the news. *If he's trying to get on the news, he may be thinking about coming after my job,* Finius thought. *Well he can bring it on.*

Finius had held his office for over twenty years and had curried favor with some of the most powerful interest groups in the country. He was a darling of the Headquarters for Arms, Rifles and Muskets (HARM) and had been awarded with the highest rating that HARM had ever conferred on a federal legislator—an A+++. He received copious contributions from industry groups and political action committees. Hence, he was not overly concerned about Cammack or any other challenger. But it was his nature to strike back, because nobody could make Finius Kochran look like a fool. Nobody.

I'm gonna teach that boy a lesson, he told himself. *He's gonna wish he'd never even thought about POOPIE.* Finius was getting impatient. He looked at the clock on his office wall, then took his gold-plated shoe-last and whammed it against his desk.

"Where's my legislation?" he howled.

A voice from outside his office said, "We're about to bring it in, sir."

"Good. I need to look it over and get my talkin' points ready."

By *look it over,* he meant that he was going to read the title. Finius, like most congressmen, never actually read any proposed bills. He was too busy for that crap. Instead, he and his colleagues just came up with a central concept and then directed other people to scribble the sundry specifics.

Finius' chief aide marched into the room holding an enormous stack of typing paper. The document totaled 372 pages and looked more like a bible than a bill. It had ten pages of *legislative intent,* which was the official congressional term for *propaganda.* It also had thirty-five pages of definitions, lest anyone be confused about what constituted a *monument.*

"Sir, here it is," the aide said, as he gently positioned the stack of papers on the congressman's desk. "It contains everything you asked for."

"What are we callin' it?" Finius asked.

"The working title is: the legislation Protecting Each Existing Publicly-Erected Enshrinement, or PEE PEE."

"I love it," Finius said. He tossed his shoe-last from one hand to the other as he glanced at the top page of the bill. "Brief me on the high points."

"Yes, sir," said the aide. "As you requested, it has six main points. First, it allows local governments to erect whatever monuments they want. Once erected, those monuments cannot be moved, molested or modified without approval from the congressman who represents the district where the monument is located or by the US Department of the Interior."

Finius rubbed his chin. "I may want to re-think that part. I ain't sure I wanna give the bureaucrats any more authority. But it's OK for now. Keep going."

The aide continued. "Thirdly, it declares that any state law that tries to deal with monuments is illegal and void."

"Now, I like that shit," Finius said.

"Then, as you asked sir, it also legalizes the sale of machine guns, appropriates $2.5 million to any national park located in Arkansas and reduces the top marginal income tax rate from fifty percent to twenty-five percent."

"Excellent," said Finius. "Any downside?"

The aide, who happened to have a law degree, looked concerned. "Well, sir, there may be some problems."

Finius stopped tossing his shoe-last and stared at the man. "Like what, exactly?"

"Well … I'm not sure that everything in here is legal, much less constitutional."

Finius stood up and pointed his shoe-last at the aide. "Listen here, son. I thought you went to law school? If Congress passes a law, then that right there makes it legal. Constitutional issues don't make a damn. Whether something is *constitutional* just means whether enough of them old bastards on the Supreme Court agree with it or not. And right now, most of them boys agree with me, so I ain't worried about that."

Actually, in 1982, the Supreme Court consisted of more than just *boys*. Finius knew that Sandra Day O'Connor had been appointed to the Court the year before, but he had opposed it, and he had not been able to break his habit of referring to the Justices as *boys*.

The aide apologized and took his leave as Finius started working on his talking points. A few minutes later, his publicity director arrived. Without saying a word, she walked behind the Congressman and began to gently brush his orange hair until it was perfectly coiffed around his ovoid noggin. Then she began to brush his cheeks with powdered base makeup. She was using beige-medium since that was the color he preferred for indoor press conferences.

As she quietly applied the makeup to his cheeks, he thought about how great he looked when his face was covered with beige-medium makeup, but he hated having to sit still while it got brushed on. He wished that there was some way that somebody could just spray his face, or even his whole body, with some sort of chemical that would make it look like he was tan. *What if it could be beige-medium and last several days,* he wondered. *I wouldn't have to worry about sweating it off.* He wondered who he could contact about trying to develop such a product. *Maybe the Plastic Manufacturers Society (PMS),* he thought. *I bet they could invent something you could spray on for a fake tan.*

He turned his head toward his publicity director and blurted, "As soon as this press conference is done, remind me to ask you about PMS," he said.

"Yes, sir," she replied as she continued with the makeup. Then she looked at the clock and said, "It's time."

Finius sprang from his chair, grabbed his new three-hundred and seventy-two page bill and looked at himself in the full-length mirror in the corner of his office. He liked what he saw.

And, by mid-afternoon on March 11, 1982, Cammack Caflin and Finius Kochran had both announced statutes about statues.

34. Judge Hatfield Talks to His Legislators

Winthrop was sitting at his desk, thinking about all the things he needed to get done when Double D pranced into his office to deliver a report.

"Congressman Kochran wants you to call him. Cammack Caflin wants you to call him. And, there's gonna be a demonstration Saturday at noon." She cocked her head, gave Winthrop a sideways glance and said, "We keep getting calls from angry people. Some of them are flat-out mean and vulgar. I'm tired of getting' them calls and, frankly, y'all don't pay me good enough to deal with that crap."

Winthrop knew how she felt. He had also received his share of angry calls. Some of the cowards would not give their names, they just screamed obscenities and made veiled threats. Sometimes he could not even tell what they wanted, other than to be loud and rude over the telephone. As he thought about those calls, he wished he could invent a way to tell who was making them. *What if there was a way to determine the identity of anyone who called you?* He envisioned a machine you could attach to your telephone that

139

would identify a caller's phone number and then display the name of the person associated with that phone. He would call it the phone-caller-finder-outer. But he did not have time to deal with crank calls. He needed a head.

"Hang in there, Double-D. We'll get all this taken care of," he said.

Double-D rolled her eyes and backed out of his office.

Great, he thought, *I've gotta call Finius and Cammack.* He dreaded having to talk to either of the legislators, so he decided to flip a coin to determine which call he would make first. He picked *heads* for Finius because of the man's big old orange head and *tails* for Cammack since he was from Paraloma, and those people were asses.

As he thought about Paraloma, he thought about the traditional coin flip that occurs at the start of every football game to determine who gets to kick off. Like everyone in town, his thoughts often drifted to the acrimonious Paraclifta-Paraloma football rivalry. The teams had battled each other for 46 straight years and each team had logged 23 wins. That was because the home team *always* won. That was because the school that hosted the game was in charge of hiring the referees. The Paraloma refs would never allow Paraclifta to win, and vice versa. The locals knew that they were doomed every odd-numbered year when the schedule required Paraclifta to face Paraloma on the road. There was really no reason to play the game at all. *It's a damn shame*, Winthrop thought. *We've had some teams that shoulda won over there, but they always get cheated.* As he obsessed on this injustice, he started thinking about his worthless legislators. *Maybe they could write a law to fix this travesty*, he thought. *Who am I kidding? Legislators would never try to get involved in high school athletics. They've got lots bigger things to worry about.*

Guided by the randomness of the coin flip, he called Cammack first.

"I had a message to call you," he said.

"Thanks," Cammack responded. "I just wanted to make sure you knew about POOPIE."

"I do," said Winthrop.

"Well, I think it's the answer. I wrote it myself and it lets you get everything fixed. With my law, nobody can prevent you from repairing a decapitated statue. Nobody."

"Much obliged," said Winthrop. "Now if I can just get these outside agitators to leave my county, I'll work on gettin' the thing fixed."

"You talkin' about the *Foray?*" Cammack asked.

"Yeah, and the OPPOSERS, and the media."

"Well, I can't speak for them other groups, but from what I know about the *Foray*, I don't think they'll give you no problem, so long as the statue stays put."

"It's stayin' put," Winthrop responded. "I can assure you of that."

Winthrop hung up and called Congressman Kochran.

"Thanks for calling me back," said Finius.

"Sure."

"I wanna make sure you know about PEEPEE," said Finius.

"I do."

"Good. Now here's the deal. You know how I believe that the feds should leave local governments alone. Well, that jackass Cammack tried to usurp my power and get the states involved in the historical monument business. That's unacceptable. My law is gonna let me, or somebody else up here in Washington, decide what happens to local monuments. That way we can keep states from interfering with that shit. And I'm gonna let you get that statue fixed since that's what you want. PEEPEE is just a way to make sure that Congress can keep states from interfering in y'all's business."

"OK," said Winthrop.

"Good. That's all I really wanted to tell you," Finius replied. "And, how's your great-grandpa doing?"

Finius did not have confidence in many people, but he absolutely loved J.D. Hatfield. A few years ago, he was attending J.D.'s one hundredth birthday party when he learned that the old man opposed change and progress of any kind. He had admired J.D. ever since.

"He's moving slow, but he's still got all his facilities," answered Winthrop.

"Great. You tell 'em I asked about 'em."

Winthrop hung up and began to pace around his office. POOPIE and PEEPEE were not going to help him. He needed his own plan and he needed it quick. He ran his hand down the back of his sans-a-belt slacks to smooth out his shirttail. One of the disadvantages of sans-a-belt slacks was that his shirttail sometimes bunched up in his crack. *I've got to talk to Paw-Paw,* he thought.

35. The Fire

Life in Paraclifta revolved around deer camps. Everyone belonged to a deer camp and would retreat to the woods when hunting season started in the first week of November. The number of deer camps in the county was second only to the number of Baptist churches.

Frogeye was very proud of his deer camp and he tried to visit it at least twice a month to make sure everything was in order. He had cut a half-pickup load of firewood from some of the limbs that had been knocked down by the tornado and he needed to carry the wood out to his camp. He was glad that Dicey had agreed to help.

They arrived at the camp just as the sun was setting and they quickly stacked the wood beneath a large boxelder tree in front of the camp house. Frogeye looked at the completed stack and estimated that it was just shy of a full rick. Firewood is measured in ricks and cords. Like most men in South Arkansas, Frogeye knew there was a state law which mandated that firewood could only be sold by the cord. It was technically illegal to sell it by the rick. In Paraclifta, three ricks equaled one cord. Frogeye thought

143

that was all silly because who would *buy* firewood in the first place? That would be like paying somebody to mow your own lawn. *Men cut their own firewood.*

While Frogeye was reminiscing about ricks, Dicey was furiously taking measurements. Every few seconds, he would shout out a result. *Fifteen inches! Thirty-eight and a half inches! Sixty inches and three of them little notches!*

Frogeye opened up the camp house and looked around. It would soon be warm enough for him to break out the bug spray to chase out the wasps and dirt-daubers. A couple of years ago, he had been victimized by a swarm of hornets. Since then, he had become very liberal in his use of bug spray.

He shut the door and went back outside. "Dicey, it's gettin' dark. Let's load up and head back to town."

After Dicey loaded up, Frogeye pointed his pickup toward Paraclifta. They traveled north on a gravel county road which wound through the woods for several miles. The road carried them by two open quarries which had supplied gravel for other county roads. The locals called these areas *gravel pits* and they were used as sites for target-shooting and beer-drinking. Sometimes amorous teenagers would go there to *park*.

When they reached the first gravel pit, Frogeye slammed on the brakes. His pickup fishtailed in the gravel before screeching to a halt. It looked like the pit was on fire. He removed his glasses and wiped their huge lenses. The fire had him bumfuzzled. *What in the hell is going on,* he wondered. As his eyes began to focus, he saw that the fire was burning in a straight line down the middle of the gravel pit. In fact, it looked like someone had piled up debris in the shape of a *number one* and then set it afire. He revved up his pickup and sped away down the gravel road. *This is not good,* he thought.

After dropping off Dicey, Frogeye went straight home and called John D.

"What's the matter?" asked John D.

"You know them crazy *Foray* people? Well, they was out at the gravel pit burning a number one. Things is gettin' out a hand around here."

"Shore sounds like it," said John D.

36. John D. Has a Dream

The Paraclifta Sawmill was the biggest employer in the county. The mill was surrounded by shotgun shacks that had been built for its workers. John D. had never married. He lived in one of the shacks in the shadow of the mill. It was the only place he had ever lived.

After graduating from high school, he served two years in the Army before coming home to work at the hardware store. He was kind, cautious and composed. One of the pervasive themes of English common law is the *reasonable man*. Jurists would apply the *reasonable man* standard to determine whether a particular act might give rise to a finding of negligence. While *reasonable man*, as a legal term, is incapable of a specific definition, it would nicely describe John D. Dalrymple. He was determined to achieve absolute reasonableness in his dealings with others.

He thought back to the conversation about people having a limited number of deer sightings. *That really applies to everything,* he thought. *Your entire life is restricted to a predetermined, finite number of events.* Days to live. Days to work. Cigarettes to smoke. *Frogeye doesn't want to waste sightings, but people really shouldn't waste anything because you never know how many days or cigarettes you have left.*

He normally had no difficulty sleeping after a long day of work, but tonight he was unsettled. For one thing, he was sad about Junior Smitherton. He wondered how the boy had gone so far astray. *What caused him to make so many bad decisions,* he wondered.

He supposed that his own life was like a slow walk through his shotgun shack. The house had three rooms, a den, bedroom and kitchen. It had a front door and a back door. His own life was three phases. He entered the world through a door that led to his childhood. Now he was in the working phase of life. If he was lucky, he would enjoy a final phase of rest and retirement before taking his final exit. He realized he was fortunate that his life-house only had three rooms. *Maybe Junior's life-house had a bunch of rooms,* he thought. *Maybe Junior was faced with lots of doors leading to bad places and he had simply opened the wrong one.*

John D. had no use for illegal drugs, but it depressed him to think about Junior being sent to jail for 40 years merely because he got caught growing some plants. In addition to Junior's predicament, John D. was also unsettled about the *Foray* pamphlets which had been strewn all over town. He knew nothing about the group, but he knew there were plenty of sketchy factions that were inclined to stir up trouble. It had never really mattered to him because Paraclifta had always been a peaceful place. Everybody knew everybody else and they treated each other with dignity and respect. He wished all these outsiders would simply leave.

He was equally annoyed about all the turmoil over the stupid statue head. It seemed like everyone in town had formed an opinion about the PIMP memorial. Some people thought it should be repaired, some thought it should be torn down, and others thought it should simply remain headless. John D. was conflicted.

He appreciated his heritage, but he was fiercely loyal. He could understand a poor boy in antebellum Arkansas being convinced to go to war to protect his home. Wars resulted from propaganda spewed by rich and powerful people who never set foot on the battlefield. Those were the men who started the Civil War, and they had done it to protect their own interests— not the interests of the poor people in Paraclifta.

He thought back to when he mustered into the Army. He had pledged an oath to protect the Constitution of the United States. He would have never violated that oath. *There was only one way to describe a soldier who violated his oath*, he thought. *Traitor. Confederate generals took the same oath I did when they became officers in the US Army. They became traitors when they took up arms against their brothers. At a minimum, they should have been imprisoned, if not executed. They didn't deserve to be memorialized by statues*, he thought. *But the rank and file who joined up after the war? Those were just poor, misguided kids who thought they were protecting their homes. They were merely pawns. Maybe a statue of one of them was ok?*

John D. knew what some of his friends thought, but he had not yet formed his own opinion. *Should I pick sides with one of the groups*, he wondered.

He started thinking about a boy he had known back in the eighth grade. They had played football and hunted together and were best friends when the boy's dad took a job down in Houston. He had never seen the boy again and he often wondered what had happened to him. He wondered if his long-lost friend would have an opinion on the statue head. He wished there was some way he could find out. *Maybe his opinion would influence mine*, he thought.

He began to wish that he could invent a machine to trace someone down and find out what they were thinking. He would call it *Trace Look*. Then he could use *Trace Look* to check on other people and see what *they* were thinking.

That would allow him to make sure that he agreed with his friends. *That's insane,* he decided. *Even if I could use* Trace Look *to see what other people were thinking, I would still make up my own mind.* Then he realized he was glad that there was nothing like *Trace Look* and that people generally kept their opinions to themselves, especially on political issues. *Reasonable people would not sit around reading* Trace Look *all day worrying about out what other folks are thinking,* he concluded.

But what about this Foray *outfit,* he wondered. *Maybe it was harmless. Maybe it resembled the Consortium and was just an excuse for a bunch of people to get together to visit and smoke cigarettes.* He hoped that was the case, and then he knocked on wood. He knew that knocking on wood only works when you do it three times, so he made a fist and hit his bedside table thrice. Then he fluffed his pillow and fell asleep.

He dreamed he was fishing at the Rolling Fork River with his friend from the eighth grade. Suddenly a galloping horse came splashing across the stream. His father was riding the horse.

"Come on boys," his dad yelled, "the folks in town want y'all to be PIMPs."

The boys followed the horse into town and got in line with a group of other young men. It seemed like everyone in town was there, including a girl he had a crush on. The Chiquapin Lady stepped forward and gave a gray PIMP jacket to each of the boys. An old man congratulated them and announced that Paraclifta was proud to be able to send 13 of its finest boys off to war. *Thirteen,* thought John D, *this is not a good idea.* A preacher gave a prayer and then everyone said, *amen.*

John D. heard a frightening roar and he looked up and saw a tornado spiraling toward downtown. He and the other boys fell on their bellies and he put his hands over his ears. When the storm passed, he stood and saw that the Chinquapin Lady had stopped moving and was wrapped in her burial shroud. When the other boys stood, they were all headless and started walking around in circles.

This is crazy, thought John D. *I'm going to the hardware store.* He reached down to the key chain on his belt loop, but there was nothing there. *Did I lose my keys?* The rest of the townsfolk still had their heads, but they were pointing at the headless PIMPs. Half of them were yelling, *no head!* The others were chanting, *new head, new head, new head!*

This is stupid, thought sleeping John D.

Day Six

37. The Consortium Gets Philosophical

Friday, March 12, 1982
5:55 a.m.
Paraclifta Hardware
Paraclifta, Arkansas

I t was five minutes before 6:00 a.m. and the Consortium's inner sanctum was already filled with second-hand cigarette smoke. Tensions were running high in town and the members of the Consortium were rattled. The head quandary was creating an even greater rift between the local diners. Meanwhile, reports about OPPOSERs and the mysterious *Foray* groups coming to town were distressing.

Yesterday, the men had seen *Foray*'s first round of propaganda leaflets. Today, they woke up to find hand-made signs all around town announcing that *Foray* was planning a demonstration at the courthouse on Saturday.

"Them *Foray* people is dangerous," Frogeye warned. "I wasn't that worried about them stupid handouts. But I'm worried now on account of them settin' a number one on fire at the gravel pit last night."

"This is getting' out a hand," said John D.

"Things was goin' haywire even before them *Foray* people showed up," noted Frogeye. "Some people are for head. Some's for new head. Some want the whole statue torn down."

"That's right," said John D. "Everybody's fussin' and pickin'" sides. I wish there was something we could do about it."

"Well, listen to this," offered Weaver. "On top of ever thing else, my wife told me that she heard that the state and the feds are tryin' to pass new laws about all this stuff. She said Congressman Kochran has done announced one that would stop anybody from removing our statue. Anybody!"

Evelray perked up when he heard this news about Congressman Kochran. Evelray had been in contact with the Congressman for the last two years because he was upset over the rampant cheating in professional wrestling. Two years ago, his favorite wrestler, Pluribus Unum, had lost *the Fight for Freedom* after a Russian wrestler cheated and used a vintage Russian shoe-last to conk him on the head. Evelray was still reeling over that injustice and had been begging the Congressman for help. He was beginning to wonder if anyone in Congress really cared about him. *Maybe they just care about big business,* he thought. *Maybe that's why my ancestors wanted to secede from the Union, because their Congressmen refused to listen to them.* Evelray knew he was being unreasonable and he wiped those thoughts from his mind. *Of course my Congressman cares about me.* "I trust Congressman Kochran," he declared.

"You ought to trust him," said Weaver. "He's a congressman, which means he's a dedicated public servant. Them guys have all kinds of ethical rules and they ain't never actin' in their own self-interests. People might disagree with 'em, but they're just aimin' to do whatever's best for their constituents."

Buddy Wayne used the only digits of his left hand to remove a cigarette from his mouth. Then he exhaled a stream of smoke and said, "I ain't interested in pickin' sides, but I don't reckon there's no reason to tear down the statue. It's been there forever. And as long as it's been up, ain't nobody really paid no attention to it. Nobody even seen that the head was missin' for several days. Nobody. That makes me think that that it don't matter if it has a head or not."

"Maybe so," said Weaver, "but them outsiders don't care nothin' about the statue nohow. They's just tryin' to get people mad at each other. Criticizing somebody on account of their race or skin color is just rude and uncalled for. It's like complainin' about another man's keychain. You don't know where them keys come from or what he uses 'em for. People should worry about their own keys—not the ones on their neighbor's belt loop."

"That don't make no sense," Buddy Wayne responded.

"I think you know what I mean," said Weaver. "It ain't right to chastise a person just cause they look different."

"When did you develop this new philosophy? Frogeye asked. "Was it before or after you'ns decided to name me *Frogeye?*"

The men laughed and Weaver clarified his position. "I ain't talkin' about commentin' on a man's looks, I'm talkin' about stereo-typin' folks based only on what tribe they belong to."

"Well. I think you're prob'ly right," Frogeye said. "But I can understand where people get upset about foreigners. I'm talkin' about people who ain't got the same values that we do. You'ns remember my Uncle Amos who lived over in Paraloma?"

The people in Paraclifta did not like the people in Paraloma. In fact, Paraclifta people disliked Paraloma people the way that the *Foray* disliked foreigners. There were several reasons for this animus, the primary one being the towns' heated, long-standing football rivalry.

Weaver took a drag from his cigarette and looked at Frogeye. "Glad to say that I don't know your uncle."

"Was he the one that was an over-the-road truck driver?" asked John D.

Frogeye nodded. "Yep. But he quit on account of the fact that they was always makin' him dead-head."

The men knew what Frogeye meant. A good trucking outfit would make sure that an over-the-road driver always had a new load after each delivery. A trucker who had to drive an empty trailer around was *dead-heading* and losing money.

"You don't never wanna dead-head," said Weaver.

"Well, I reckon our Rebel soldier has a dead head," John D. observed.

Frogeye continued, "Anyway, a few years ago, Uncle Amos took a vacuum cleaner engine and reversed it. Then he used the hose to blow all the leaves outta his yard. He called his gadget a *leaf lifter*. He started braggin' about inventin' it and then he started workin' on a way to turn it into a backpack so's you could walk around and get rid of leaves faster than by usin' a rake. Bout a year later, ever body started selling leaf blowers. Amos was convinced that some Jews had done stole his idea and got rich off it. He was mad about it all the way to his grave. If he was still alive, he'd a prob'ly joined an outfit like the *Foray*."

John D. rubbed his forehead. "I reckon that's why most people get in them groups. People's always lookin' to blame somebody else for their own problems. Yore uncle shoulda moved quicker. He shoulda bought a patent or hired somebody to start selling his *leaf lifters*. But he got beat to the punch so he blamed somebody else. Truth is, nobody ever wants to take responsibility for their own mistakes."

"Nobody," said Buddy Wayne.

Frogeye explained, "I ain't tryin' to sound anti-symmetrical, and I ain't in favor of no hate groups, I'm just sayin' that there's two sides to ever story."

"Sorry," said Evelray, "but I don't trust foreigners. I sure don't trust Russians. And, I'm proud we got leaders who don't go around trusting Russians."

"I heard that," said Frogeye.

Evelray was not finished. "And I ain't never buying no Jap car. You know how the Japs treated our boys in World War II? I'm tellin' y'all right now, I'm just thankful that we live in a country where we can manufacture whatever we need and we ain't gotta rely on no foreigners to build our stuff fer us."

"Maybe so, but what I'm sayin' is that it ain't gonna be no good at all if them *Foray* people have a demonstration tomorrow," said Buddy Wayne.

"Maybe nobody'll show up," said John D.

"You know better'n that. Ever body in town will be there," predicted Buddy Wayne.

"Well, I ain't got the answer, but I wish there was somethin' we could do," said John D.

Buddy Wayne blew a stream of cigarette smoke toward the ceiling. "On one hand, we ought to just ignore them trouble-makers," he said as he held up his hand that only had one finger. "On the other hand, somebody needs to stand up to 'em," he said as he raised up his three-fingered hand. "It's a classic *Occam's razor* situation."

"I think you mean a *Sophie's choice,*" said Weaver.

"He means a *Catch-22*," said John D.

"Nope," Frogeye interjected, "it's called a *Buridan's ass*. It's where you can't make a decision between two evenly-matched options."

Buddy Wayne lowered his mangled hands and looked at Frogeye. "I think you're a bumblin' ass," he muttered.

Weaver had heard enough. He stubbed out his cigarette and stood up. "Hey, John D., reckon y'all got any decent leaf blowers? I been thinkin' about tryin' one out."

John D. said, "Shore do. We got three different kinds." He winked at Frogeye and said, "And the cheapest one comes outta Japan. Come on up here and I'll show 'em to ya. I need to open the store anyhow."

Weaver followed John D. to the front of the store as Frogeye pouted and took his last swig of coffee. The Consortium was adjourned.

38. Finius Prevails

Finius hated reading newspapers. It was no fun and he was a busy man. But he knew he had to generally stay abreast of current events and he always wanted to know whenever his name appeared in print. Consequently, he routinely ordered one of his aides to read several newspapers each morning and then provide him a daily briefing, not to exceed five minutes. It was time for today's briefing. He liked to pace around his office during his news briefings because it kept him alert, and made it less likely that he might fall asleep.

He was walking in a circle around his desk as his aide delivered the news.

Aide: "Sir, here is today's report: President Reagan has banned oil imports from Libya because he says Libya is sponsoring terrorism. And, there's a report about members of Congress who want to freeze our levels of nuclear weapons. You voted against that. A new report says that Reagan has been providing millions of dollars in secret financial aid to groups in Nicaragua who want to overthrow their government. The Food and Drug Administration is demanding a recall of some baby food ….

159

Finius stopped pacing and interrupted the aide. "The *Food and Drug Administration*," he sneered. "Those worthless bureaucrats. I knew they'd be pullin' shit like this after they got all them food-labeling laws passed."

Finius had been a fierce opponent of laws requiring labels on manufactured food. That was the main reason he had picked up support from the Society of Cobblers and Merchants (SCAM).

"May I continue, Sir?" asked the addled aide.

"Yeah, but speed it up. I need to work on something productive."

"OK." The aide said as he referred to his notes. "The Chairman of the Joint Chiefs says that we will not send troops to fight communists in El Salvador. And, finally, Senator Williams resigned over that Abscam business."

Finius knew all about Abscam, the FBI sting operation that had led to convictions of several elected officials for bribery and corruption. He stopped pacing again. "Well, none of that shit is relevant to anything that we're trying to do in this office. Was there anything in there about my statue law?"

"We've had some reporters call about it, but I haven't seen any news articles on it yet. Several other Congressmen are asking about it and most of the ones from the South may be talking to you to see if they can join on as co-sponsors."

"Good," said Finius. "I want that shit in the news. I want people talking about how I'm showin' my support for local government by preventin' local government from doing things that I oppose. Anything else to report news-wise?"

"No, sir," the aide said.

"Then go on about your business and see if you can't gin up some interest in PEE PEE."

The aide nodded and took his leave.

Finius returned to his desk and plopped down in his luxury office chair. He detected a presence and looked up to see one of his secretaries timidly peeping around the edge of the doorway. She looked like a nervous squirrel considering a leap onto a hanging bird feeder.

"What's the matter with you?" he barked.

"It's PMS again," she replied.

"Hmm," said Finius. "Normally PMS only bothers me about once a month. ... But I'm happy to talk to 'em. Shut that door on the way out!"

Finius leaned back in his chair, stared at the ceiling, and balanced his shoe-last on his forehead. The gold-plated exterior felt cool and comfortable against his skin. Keeping his head perfectly still, he carefully picked up his telephone handset and slowly brought it up to his ear. He managed to get the telephone properly situated between his shoulder and his jowl without allowing the shoe-last to slide off his head. This made him smile for the first time all day.

"This is Finius," he said.

After there was no response, he tried again. "This is Finius!"

He then realized that he had forgotten to press the blinking button that allowed the call to be transferred to his office phone. As he lurched forward to mash the button, the gold-plated shoe-last tumbled from his forehead to the floor.

"Sonofabitch!" he grunted.

He picked up the shoe last and brushed it against his pants leg. The last thing he wanted was a dusty shoe-last. Satisfied with his polishing effort, he mashed the blinking button and returned the telephone headset to his ear so he could talk to the PMS director.

"Sorry to keep you waiting," Finius said, "I've been extra-busy around here today. Fact is, I got more poured out than I can smooth over."

"No problem," said the director, "I can only imagine how much you have to deal with."

"Well, I wasn't expecting a call from y'all today. What can I do for you?"

"You've already done it," the director answered. "I don't know exactly what you did, but WASTE called and they've put in an order for plastic soap dispensers for every federal office in D.C. Our members are about to make a fortune!"

"That's what I'm talking about," said Finius.

"Well, needless to say, we're extremely pleased. Our political action committee met this morning and I think you're gonna be happy with the next contribution you get from us. We're also gonna deliver you a personal, gold-plated soap dispenser for your office."

Finius was flattered. "I love PMS," he said. "Y'all let me know if you need anything else."

He hung up the telephone and started spinning his shoe-last again. Truth be told, he did not give a rat's ass about what happened in Paraclifta, but he cared deeply about catering to his supporters. While other people were getting stirred up over a statue, he could quietly use his influence to help his friends line their pockets. Nobody made any money off a statue, but there was plenty of money to be made off government contracts. *Damn,* he thought, *I really ought to run for President.*

39. Junior Cuts a Deal

rlen was anxious. Yesterday, he had been fretting over the dozens of calls his office had received from people upset about *Foray*'s offensive pamphlets. Now he was worrying about the signs plastered all over town that advertised a *Foray* rally tomorrow. He knew that Winthrop, Cammack and Finius were focused on the politics surrounding the broken statue, but none of them seemed to be focused on keeping the peace. Arlen was hell-bent on keeping the peace in Paraclifta. He was preparing to brief his deputies when he received a call from Junior Smitherton. *I don't have time to talk to a drug dealer who's out on bail,* he thought as he picked up the phone.

"What do you need, Junior?" the sheriff asked.

"Well, I need to talk to you. I can't do no forty years. That ain't right."

"You shoulda thought about that before you took a notion to start growing dope," said Arlen.

"I ain't sayin' I shouldn't be punished … but forty years?" Junior sounded like he was on the verge of tears again.

163

Arlen stood firm. "Son, I don't write the laws. Very smart men in Little Rock and Washington take care of that. Brilliant men. They're honest, public servants and all they do is look out for the health and safety of us regular folks. Hell, they spend hours and hours studying issues and thinkin' 'bout things. They talk to experts and scientists and it takes 'em months to come up with the idea for a law. Then they work on it and they read it and change it and then read it again. Them smart men spend a helluva lot a time before they go passin' a new law that affects the rest of us. So, when they decide that growing dope can get you forty years in the pen, then that's the end of it. My job's just to enforce the law. My hands are tied, if you know what I mean."

"What can I do for some help?" pleaded Junior.

Arlen hated drug dealers and this had turned into his department's biggest case. At the same time, he genuinely believed Junior was harmless. As much as he wanted to help the boy, he could not envision any justification for a lenient sentence.

He told Junior, "First off, marijuana is killin' people and ruinin' this country. There ain't no excuse for gettin' involved with that poison, and you oughta' know better. Now sometimes, if you have some helpful information, like somebody you could snitch on, that could help in a situation like this. But accordin' to you, this was all your own dope. So, I can't see no way you can help yourself. I reckon you just need to get yourself a good lawyer and hope for the best."

"OK," said Junior. "But let me ask you something. Everybody in town is talkin' about the damn statue, right? Well, what if I could help with that?"

"What are you talkin' about?" asked Arlen. He could not imagine that Junior could do anything that would help mitigate the monument mayhem.

Junior decided to show his cards. "Hypothetically speakin' …
what if I could get you a certain head that ever body seems to be
interested in?"

Arlen was engrossed. After a brief pause he said, "Well, that's
a horse of a different stripe. That right there might be the kind of
thing that could shore 'nuff help you out."

40. The King of the County Consults with His Advisor

Winthrop kept a Bible in his office and frequently turned to it for inspiration. He was sitting at his desk reading Daniel, Chapter Two.

He was reading about the King of Babylonia who had been troubled by dreams. One of his dreams involved an enormous, dazzling statue which was awesome in appearance. Winthrop read these verses:

> The head of the statue was made of pure gold, its chest and arms of silver, its belly and thighs of bronze, its legs of iron, its feet partly of iron and partly of baked clay. While you were watching, a rock was cut out, but not by human hands. It struck the statue on its feet of iron and clay and smashed them. Then the iron, the clay, the bronze, the silver and the gold were all broken to pieces and became like chaff on a threshing floor in the summer.

Winthrop was captivated as he read about the king's consultations with magicians, enchanters, sorcerers and astrologers who could not divine the dream. The king was so frustrated that he threatened to kill the men. Then Daniel was brought forward

166

and was able to explain the dream's meaning. Daniel told the King that each of the statue's substances represented different kingdoms of varying strength. And if a kingdom is not united, like a mixture of iron and clay, it can be broken to pieces.

Winthrop was deep in meditation. He considered himself the king of Paraclifta. *The statue in my kingdom had been damaged, but not by human hands. Is my own kingdom coming to an end,* he wondered. *Not if I can get the people in my kingdom to stay united.*

Winthrop did not have access to magicians, enchanters, sorcerers and astrologers, but he did have his own learned consultant—his Paw-Paw. He set down his Bible, closed his door and called his great-grandpa. He listened to ring after ring while he waited on J.D. to pick up the phone. As he waited, he wished he could just talk on the phone without having to cram the receiver up to his head. He wished that there was some sort of headset or wireless device he could stick in his ear so he could pace around his office without being tethered to a telephone cord. But he did not have time to think about nifty communication advancements, he needed to talk to his Paw-Paw.

A few minutes later, J.D. finally answered the call.

"Paw-Paw, I need advice again."

"Have you got daddy's head fixed?" J.D. asked.

"No, but I'm aimin' to. Right now, we got all kinds of problems. There's a group what's come to town that's tryin' to stir up trouble. They're gonna hold some kinda rally at the courthouse tomorrow, and I don't like it one bit. There's probably gonna be TV cameras everywhere and I'm afraid it may turn bad. I just want to try to keep everybody united," Winthrop explained.

"Is it them racist bastards?" asked J.D.

"Yep."

"OK," said J.D. "I've dealt with them types before. All they wanna do is try to spook people and stir up a fuss. You can't expect folks to ignore 'em, 'cause it'll be a Saturday and everybody's gonna show up to see what happens. But what you do is, you take the attention away from 'em."

"How do I do that?" Winthrop asked.

"You beat 'em to the punch. About half an hour before they're plannin' their rally, you put on yer own little shindig. Schedule an official announcement to talk about what all the county's gonna do to help re-build them businesses and help the folks that got their houses banged up. Say that you're gonna get state and federal money and that you're startin' a fund where people can donate to the cause. Tell 'em that the county's gonna help them rebuild bigger 'n better, *blah, blah, blah*. It ain't even gotta be true. Just say some positive shit like that and everybdy'll get happy and move along before there's any kind a protest."

"That's a great idea, Paw-Paw."

"It'll work. And throw in some big words. Voters love that shit. And listen here, have a preacher there to open it up with a prayer. That'll tone things down."

"Good idea," said Winthrop. "I know the perfect one. There's a new preacher in town. He ain't been here long enough to make nobody mad yet. He's even given me some help on some political decisions."

"Hmpf," said J.D. "Preachers ain't got no place in politics. Ever body knows that. And, remember this—don't never let a preacher tell you how to vote and don't never let a politician tell you how to pray."

"Good advice," said Winthrop.

"There's two kinds of people who make me nervous: preachers and people who back into parking spaces."

"I heard that," said Winthrop.

"And here's another idea. Get you a colored person to make some comments. And you might even consider gettin' a cripple up there with you. When them TV people see our county judge taking the stage with a preacher, a minority and somebody who's all gimped up, that's all they'll be interested in and them outsiders will see that it's time for them to move along and leave us be. And at the same time, it'll be some good media coverage for you. Voters love that shit."

Winthrop was very encouraged. "Thanks, Paw-Paw. You're an absolute genius."

"Listen to me," J.D. said as he launched into a list of his ongoing grievances, "these fringe groups are just like ever body else. They got some kinda agenda and they wanna force radical changes on us. If they get their way, they'll be forcin' people to get vaccinations and dictatin' what we can teach our kids. Mark my words, it won't be long 'til they legalize dope and outlaw cigarettes."

J.D. was convinced that various groups of outsiders were constantly conspiring to attack his way of life. It was his default position. Winthrop had endured these tirades for years and did not want to listen to another one today.

"I really appreciate it, Paw-Paw, but I got to go."

"Don't mention it," said J.D. "And one more thing, just in case my plan don't work out, I'd recommend that you put in a call to the National Guard just in case."

Now Winthrop felt discouraged again. *Do we really need the National Guard?* he wondered. He said goodbye to his great-grandpa and then yelled at his secretary.

"D, get me the National Guard on the phone!"

This is really getting out of hand, he thought.

41. Cammack Faces the Press

Cammack had embarked on the day in a chimerical mood. He was still delighted about writing his first law and looking forward to promoting POOPIE. His only regret about his press conference was that he had forgotten to pack it with some of his supporters and he had neglected to have a preacher lead it off with a prayer. *Live and learn,* he thought.

Shortly after arriving at Cafflin Insurance agency, which was located in a boring brick building in downtown Paraloma, his day took a drastic turn for the worse. First, he picked up his copy of the state's largest newspaper, *The Arkansas Insider,* and saw a front-page article about the statue controversy that barely mentioned the law he had drawn up. Instead, it focused on how Paraclifta had been littered with racist literature by an extremist group known as the *Foray.* Even worse, the newspaper criticized Cammack for calling the *Foray* members *very fine people.*

Now he was sitting at his desk staring at a pile of paper that was thicker than the Little Rock phone book. The document was a copy of Congressman Kochran's new federal law, which

170

had just been dropped off by a courier. After glancing at the first
few pages of the legislation, Cammack quickly understood that
he had been seriously out-maneuvered. Finius's bill had
covenants and commands, definitions and decrees, edicts and
explanations, findings and footnotes, preambles and paragraphs,
and sections and sub-sections. Each page was bursting with
clever calligraphy. He did not understand much of it, but as he
stared at the pages, he knew it was a legislative masterpiece.
Cammack was crestfallen. *Why did I even try?* he wondered. *I'm
not a real legislator.*

His secretary interrupted his self-loathing by announcing that
a reporter from New York was on the telephone. This lifted his
spirits a little. *People up in New York wanna talk to me? Maybe I can
get this turned around,* he thought.

"This is State Representative Cafflin," he told the reporter.
"What can I do for you?"

The reporter asked Cammack if he would confirm that he had
referred to the *Foray* as *very fine people.*

"Well, actually I got a little misquoted," Cammack explained.
"I was talking about people who got strong feelings about that
Rebel monument. Whether you like it or not, the people in
Paraclifta are proud of the PIMPs. I've talked to lots of people in
the military and they all brag on the PIMPs and everything they
stood for."

"Sir, I'm asking if you said that the people who passed out racist
leaflets are *very fine people?*" asked the reporter.

Cammack was getting frustrated. He could tell that this Yankee
reporter was trying to trip him up. "Just because people want to
protect PIMPs, it don't mean that they're racist. If you look at what
I said, I answered that question perfectly."

The reporter had heard enough. "Thank you for your time,"
she said.

Cammack hung up the phone, grabbed his copy of Finius's legislation and threw it at the wall. "Poopie!" he yelled as he watched 372 sheets of paper flutter to the ground.

42. Sheriff Dingler Plots a Plan

Sheriff Dingler had the head.

After some shrewd negotiating, Junior produced the missing head in exchange for the reduction of his criminal charge. Junior had explained that after he had been released on bond, he had gone back home and taken a stroll through the cow pasture behind his trailer house. He recalled thinking it was odd to be sober and taking a walk. He was just wandering around trying to clear his mind when he tripped, fell and came face to face with the severed head of a Confederate soldier.

Thanks to the growing unease in the community, the head turned out to be a powerful bargaining tool. Junior offered to produce the head subject to one condition—that he be spared any jail time. Arlen agreed and promised to drop Junior's charge from *manufacturing* to simple *possession*. Once the plea bargain was consummated, Junior, who was a first-time offender, became eligible for probation in lieu of jail time.

Now, Junior could sleep at night and Arlen had the head. While Junior had used the head as a get-out-of-jail-free card, Arlen hoped to use it as a peace-making tool.

Arlen placed the PIMP head on his desk and began to devise his scheme. As he formulated his plan, he performed an inspection of the solid chunk of pale marble. He saw no evidence of cracks or structural defects, but noticed acidic stains on the top of the coonskin cap. He presumed the stains were the result of decades of bird droppings. The entire neck was intact and the soldier had a stern face with fierce eyes beneath brushy eyebrows. As he stared into the PIMP's face, he thought it resembled J.D. Hatfield.

The inspection was cut short when he heard Winthrop's voice in the hallway. He quickly concealed the head by cramming it beneath his desk just as Winthrop stepped into his office.

"Sheriff," said Winthrop nervously, "I need to talk to you."

"Sure," said Arlen.

"I've been worried about all these outsiders, and now that *Foray* bunch is planning a rally or some nonsense at the courthouse tomorrow."

"I wouldn't worry too much about that," said Arlen.

"How come?"

"Well, for starters, them *Foray* guys is probably just a bunch of loudmouths. Most people have done ignored them propaganda pamphlets they strowed all over town. Once they get down here, and actually look around, they'll probably leave out of sheer boredom. Hell, they scheduled an early morning rally, which means they won't have time to get liquored up. And since we're in a dry county, there won't be nothin' for them rascals to do after they get here. I say we just let 'em march around and pop off at the mouth for a few minutes, and then they'll mosey off to raise hell someplace else. Probably in Oklahoma."

"Well, you may be right, but I don't want no trouble. So, I wanted to let you know that I'm plannin' to set up a little program *before* they get here. I'm gonna talk about the storm cleanup and

I'm thinkin' about seein' if we can get the high school football boys up here to help with some of that."

"That's not a bad idea," responded Arlen.

"And I've also asked for the National Guard to be here, just in case," Winthrop said meekly.

"I really don't think that's gonna be necessary," said Arlen, "but I'll be happy to coordinate with 'em."

"Thanks, sheriff. I really appreciate it." Winthrop said quietly.

Arlen had not wanted to share his plan with Winthrop, but he did want some more information.

"Judge," he said, "since you've got us lookin' for that missing head, can you give me a description of it?"

"Not really," said Winthrop as he looked away from the sheriff. "I'm sad to say it, but I never really paid much attention to it all these years. I do know it was one of the PIMPs, so I reckon it'd look like a handsome young white man."

"Hmmm," said Arlen. "Well, hang in there, Judge. I got a feelin' that things are gonna turn out OK."

Winthrop stood, hiked up his sans-a-belt slacks and said goodbye.

As a longtime lawman and master-interrogator, Arlen was left with the distinct impression that Winthrop had not been entirely truthful about the head.

43. John D. Gets a Haircut

John D. needed a haircut, but more importantly, he needed information. Only one place in town had more news on local affairs than the Consortium and that place was Joe's Barber Shop. When John D. closed the hardware store for lunch, he decided to go to Joe's and kill two birds with one stone.

The town's only barbershop was in a square portable building which housed a lone barber's chair surrounded by mirrors attached to each of the four interior walls. Joe was always open during the lunch hour because everybody in town, other than the very young and the very old, worked on weekdays and lots of men liked to squeeze in a haircut during their lunch break.

Joe was sitting in his barber chair reading a newspaper when John D. arrived. John D. was always pleased when he saw someone reading a newspaper. He read at least one newspaper every day and he strongly believed that all reasonable people had an obligation to read the paper and keep abreast of current events.

Joe was wearing his traditional haircutting outfit which consisted of blue jeans and a white tee shirt under a white apron coated with an agglomeration of second-hand whiskers and hair. He had broad shoulders and a bounteous beer belly. Weaver had once suggested that Joe looked like a black diamond watermelon had been stuffed up his tee shirt.

Joe had given haircuts to practically every grown man in town and he was proud that he even cut his own hair. His personal hairdo was a tight, Ivy League crew cut, parted on the right. His hair always looked fantastic from straight ahead. But despite the array of mirrors in his shop, he had never been able to get it squared up neatly in the back. Whenever people looked at him from behind, they always thought he was tilting his head from right to left even if his head was in its normal position.

Joe hopped out of the barber chair and motioned for John D. to take a seat. He popped a chair cloth, draped it over John D.'s chest and fastened it around his neck. Now John D. looked like he was wearing a cape backwards.

"How's it going, John D.?"

"Not bad," John D. replied, "as far as I know."

"I heard that. Y'all didn't have no damage from that storm, did ya?"

"Nope, we got lucky."

"Yeah. I reckon we're all lucky that nobody got hurt."

"Nobody," John D. agreed.

"And it looks like they're startin' to make some progress with the cleanup." Joe said as he furiously snipped away. He was already making some serious progress with John D.'s haircut.

"What've you heard about this head situation?" asked John D.

Hearing the question, Joe froze and stared at his reflection in the front mirror of his shop. That mirror reflected the image of Joe staring into another mirror which reflected the image of Joe staring into another mirror, and so on. While Joe stared into the infinity of images of himself staring into a mirror, John D. stared at the back of Joe's hair and tried to figure out if Joe was tilting his head or not.

After an uneasy moment of silence, Joe said to his reflection in the mirror, "It's bad business is what it is. Everybody is arguing and upset about it." Joe unfroze and turned to look at John D. "The cafes are split on what to do," he said as he chopped his scissors in the air. "That silly state representative from Paraloma wants to get right in the middle of it." Chop. "Our congressman wants to get right in the middle of it." Chop. "Some batch of racists is threatenin' to hold a rally." Chop. "And, some do-gooder legal outfit sent a lawyer down here who's threatenin' to sue everybody." Chop.

"Dang," said John D. "A lawyer is the last thing we need around here."

"I heard that," said Joe, resuming his haircutting.

"Do you got a feeling for what most people think ought to happen?"

Joe stopped trimming again. "Not really. *Somethin'* just needs to happen fast. If somebody'd just make a decision, no matter what it is, I reckon that'd end all the fussin'. But it's like a lotta things. Nobody wants to step up."

"Nobody," agreed John D. "But I hope that somebody gets it figured out soon."

"Me, too," said Joe the barber. "If they don't, I'm afraid that the Chinquapin Lady might drop graveyard dead."

"Why is that?" asked John D.

"Well, she stopped me on the sidewalk yesterday and said she'd read one of them racist letters that was thrown out all over town. She said that pamphlet helped her figure out what caused the tornado."

"Oh yeah, what was that?"

Joe explained, "According to her, our tornado was caused by Jewish space lasers."

"Good Lord," said John D. "I guess she's finally gone off the deep end. I reckon somebody should send her to the crazy house."

"You're probably right," Joe said. "Nobody in their right mind would ever blame a natural disaster on a space laser."

"Nobody," said John D.

"Anybody who says things that crazy needs to be sent to a psychologist," Joe said.

"What do you think they should do with the statue?" asked John D.

"I don't give a rat's ass what they do," answered Joe. "We got a lot bigger problems, like gettin' things cleaned up, gettin' us a new drug store built and gettin' rid of dopers, like Junior Smitherton. That's what the county needs to be thinkin' about."

"I heard that," said John D.

44. Winthrop Plans a Shindig

Winthrop was moving with alacrity. He was planning his own official shindig to take place before the *Foray* rally. He was going to take the wind out of their sails. He had already lined up the town's new preacher to open the ceremony and he had convinced Dorinda to say a few words. He was still thinking about whether he wanted to include a cripple, but he was prepared to make some positive comments and then he hoped that the crowd would disperse and that would be that. Just in case, he had gone ahead and ordered up some National Guard troops. *Better safe than sorry,* he thought.

Since the event was taking place on a Saturday, he thought he might as well see if he could get the high school involved. He had called the high school to leave a message for Toehead Faulkner. Toehead was the head football coach, which meant he was also the athletic director, which meant he was one of the most important people in the county. Toehead looked like a high school football coach. He was stocky and block-headed with unruly, pale-blond hair.

Winthrop was thinking about football again when Toehead finally called him back.

"What's goin' on, Judge?" he asked.

Winthrop said, "I should be asking you that. How's the track team looking?"

"We got a bunch out, but ain't none of 'em very fast," Toehead replied. "But the football squad should be ready to roll this fall. We're gonna beat Paraloma's ass, I can guarantee you that."

Winthrop smiled. He knew that track and field had been invented merely to occupy the time between basketball and football seasons. He also knew that Paraclifta was hosting Paraloma next football season which truly did guarantee a win for the home team. "Glad to hear it. Reckon you could get some of your players to come downtown tomorrow? I thought I might brag on 'em a little and then see if they could help with some of the tornado cleanup."

"Be glad to," Toehead said. "I was actually thinkin' about that before you called. It'd be good for the boys to lend a hand. I seen y'all done hauled off a lot of the wreckage. Where'd ya take it all?"

"The road crew has been carryin' it out to one of the gravel pits." Winthrop said. "They burned a bunch of it out there last night."

"Oh," said Toehead. "Well, I betcha I can get my guys up there tomorrow. Reckon what time do you need 'em?"

"Let's say 9:00," Winthrop answered.

The men ended their call and Winthrop stood and hiked up his slacks. *I don't know if this is gonna work, but if nothing else, we're fixin' to beat Paraloma's ass this fall,* he thought.

45. Weaver Gets in on the Plan

Weaver was at home making a trial run with the new leaf blower he had bought at the Paraclifta hardware store. He thought it worked fine. His only complaint was that it lacked a cup holder. He thought it would be much handier if it had a spot where he could set his glass of iced tea. It was difficult to hold the blower with one hand and then maneuver a cigarette *and* a glass of iced tea with the other, but he was doing his best.

He was brooding because his wife had given him grief over the purchase. "Weaver, you already have 53 firearms, and now you have this thing that looks like a stove-pipe bazooka. Why are you so fond of crap like this?" she had asked.

This is what he wanted to say to her: *This thing gives me a chance to go outside and be by myself for a while, away from all your naggin'.* But here is how he actually replied: *Because I think it'll come in handy, dear, and* John D. *made me a really good deal on it.*

He was already a little perturbed with his wife. She had started buying liquid hand soap. Now, instead of just grabbing a manly bar of soap, he had to pump a plastic container to dispense a flowery-smelling gel into his hands. It made no sense to him. It was more expensive and he doubted that it made his hands any cleaner. He halfway suspected it was just another unnecessary excuse for plastic. It seemed wasteful and foolish. *Why is there so much plastic,* he wondered. *Who's behind this? The next thing you know, they'll start putting regular-old water in plastic bottles and people will drink that instead of just pouring tap water into a cup. Well,* he thought, *if she can buy fancy hand soap, I shouldn't feel bad about buying a Japanese leaf blower.*

He loved his wife and he knew he could not manage the county's greatest vegetable garden without her. But he wanted to ask her why she was so fond of their telephone. It seemed like she was always on the phone talking to her friends. She went straight to the phone anytime she got wind of a scandal. Recently the talk had all been centered around Junior Smitherton's arrest or the broken statue.

He and his friends did not talk on the phone all day. They actually took the time to sit down together at the Consortium. *It must be nice,* he thought, *sitting around gossiping with other women on the telephone all day.* He aimed his new leaf blower at a pile of sweet gum balls. He mashed the throttle and the balls bounded off into the distance, leaving billows of yellowish pollen and dust. He deftly kept his iced tea to the side to protect it from airborne contaminants. As his machine sent miscellaneous detritus into flight, he continued to think about his wife's compulsion to talk to her friends about every little thing. *They could make a TV show about those women,* he thought. *They could call it Paraclifta Housewives. But that would never work,* he concluded. *Nobody would ever sit around and watch a TV show about random housewives. Nobody.*

His daydreaming was interrupted when he saw his wife on the porch waving her arms. She looked like she was trying to bring a plane in for a landing. He killed the leaf blower's engine and said, "What?"

"The sheriff needs you to call him!" she said. "Hurry up and do it so you can tell me what's going on."

Good grief, thought Weaver. He set down the leaf blower, took a swig of iced tea and a drag of his cigarette and headed inside. Sheriff Dingler answered on the first ring.

"Sheriff, this is Weaver."

"Thanks for calling me back. How's it going?"

"I can't complain, but sometimes I still do," Weaver answered. "Also, Frogeye is a little agitated that you ain't never asked him to be a deputy."

For a moment, the Sheriff debated whether he could really use Frogeye. *I wonder if he could use them thick-ass glasses to locate trace evidence at crime scenes,* he thought. He decided he would think about it later.

"I'll keep that in mind," he said. "But that's not what I called about." Arlen explained that Junior had found the missing head and had given it up in exchange for a plea bargain. "Reckon the Consortium can take that head and repair the memorial at the courthouse?" he asked.

"I reckon the Consortium could fix damn near anything," answered Weaver.

"That's what I was hoping you'd say," said Arlen. "I wanna give you this thing and ask y'all to go up there tonight and see if you can get it back on. And don't tell nobody," said Arlen. "Nobody."

Weaver promised the men would give it a try. He was relieved to find out that Junior had been granted leniency.

When he hung up the phone, his wife was looking for answers. "What's going on?" she asked.

"I can't talk about it right now," he replied. And then he got in his pickup and drove to the hardware store.

46. The Consortium Conducts a Clandestine Operation

John D. was acquainted with every hardware implement known to mankind. Evelray had attained the rank of master plumber. Weaver was an expert electrician, owned 53 firearms and could grow any vegetable that was adaptable to the climate of south Arkansas. Frogeye was an amateur meteorologist who knew every acre of the county. Buddy Wayne had spent a lifetime building things in Paraclifta and could identify every species of tree in the state. Three of the men had high school diplomas, one had a GED, and all of them had served in the Army. But despite their many skills, accomplishments and experience, no one in this talented group had ever performed any work on a marble statue.

The courthouse square was deserted when Frogeye rolled his pickup into the parking spot closest to the Confederate memorial. Evelray was in the passenger seat gently cradling the Rebel soldier's head in his lap. John D., Buddy Wayne and Weaver were couched in the bed of the truck with a ladder and an assortment of hand tools.

185

It was a cool night and the men were appropriately dressed for their mission, outfitted in dark flannel shirts. Weaver was wearing a Headquarters for Arms Rifles and Muskets hat which bore the HARM logo and read: *I'm a HARMer*. The other men were wearing camouflage hunting caps.

Under the cover of darkness, the men disembarked from the pickup like a team of well-trained special weapons and tactics officers. Evelray used both arms to hold the soldier's head against his gut as he and his friends trotted toward the statue. They looked like a squad of football players leading a fullback across the goal line.

When they reached the base of the monument, they instinctively formed a semi-circle while Evelray gently placed the head on the ground. "That head's pretty heavy," he observed.

"I'll tell you something else," said Weaver, "the face on that head shore does favor J.D. Hatfield "

"We ain't got time to admire the damn head," John D. said in frustration. "Let's get it back where it belongs."

At that point, the men realized that they had forgotten to unload the ladder from Frogeye's truck.

"Somebody go get the ladder," said John D.

"Not me," protested Evelray. "I'm wore out from carryin' that head."

"I'll go get it," said Weaver.

As they waited for the ladder, the other men fired up cigarettes and admired the statue. It had an ominous glow, like the ancient headstones in the city cemetery.

"I bet it was a chore to carve this thing out of a big chunk a rock," observed Buddy Wayne. "We don't build things as good as they did back in the olden days."

"If people was to build a statue nowadays, they'd probably just make it out of plastic," Frogeye said sourly.

"I heard that," Weaver said as he returned with the ladder. He extended it until the top rung was resting against the soldier's chest and then used his feet to scotch the ladder's bottom legs.

With the ladder properly situated, Buddy Wayne wrapped a tool belt around his overalls and began to climb. When he reached the summit, he took the only finger on his left hand and rubbed it around on the top of the soldier's neck. Luckily, he discovered a smooth surface. It had been a clean break. He removed a square sheet of high-grit sandpaper and began to polish.

While Buddy Wayne was preparing the neck, Evelray pointed a small flashlight at the statue's inscription and began to read it aloud: "This monument is dedicated to the brave men of the Paraclifta Infantry Men Platoon. We will always remember the PIMP's unselfish dedication to their glorious cause. The principles for which they fought live eternally. Pimpin' ain't easy."

"I heard that," said Frogeye.

"No doubt. They was some brave men," said Weaver.

"No tellin' what they musta went through," said Frogeye.

"You know who needs a statue?" Evelray asked.

"No, but I reckon you're gonna tell us," John D. replied.

Evelray was proud to tell them. "Pluribus Unum," he said. "He's the best athlete in the world and he's a true American."

"Well who could argue with that?" Weaver asked sarcastically. Unfortunately, the other members of the Consortium did not share Evelray's devotion to professional wrestling.

"You know what else," continued Evelray, "Pluribus Unum should run for President."

"Was he in the service?" asked Weaver.

"I reckon so. He's a man, ain't he," concluded Evelray.

"Well, I'd need to know. I can't vote for somebody for president if he ain't served his country," Weaver explained.

Atop the ladder, Buddy Wayne continued his repair efforts. Satisfied with his sand-papering, he was now using a soft cloth to clean the head reattachment site. Back on the ground, the Consortium continued their discussion.

"Weaver's right," said Frogeye. "Lots a people may not wanna serve, but they have to when the nation depends on it." He pointed at the Rebel soldier's head, which was looking up at them from the ground. "This guy right here probably had better things to do, but he grabbed a rifle and joined up. He did his part."

"He did it for Paraclifta," added Weaver. "That's what it's all about. You step up to protect your land, your family and your neighbors."

"Not serving is un-American," said John D. "It'd be like refusing to get vaccinated during a pandemic."

"Even though the PIMPs were on the losing side, you still gotta respect them for their service," said Weaver. "So, if your man Pluto weren't in the service, then I ain't votin' for him."

"It's Pluribus," said Evelray. "Like it says on a quarter."

"I thought coins said, *in God we trust,*" said Weaver.

"They do, but they also say Pluribus Unum." Evelray replied. "And I'm gonna find out if he was in the service, but I'm sure that he was."

"You know something?" Weaver asked. "I don't mind payin' a quarter for a bag of chips, but I expect to get at least a quarter's worth of chips when I open the bag."

"I heard that," said Frogeye.

The Consortium's banter was interrupted by Buddy Wayne's announcing that he was ready for the head. Weaver, the tallest member of the Consortium, climbed to the second step of the ladder and carefully lifted the head into Buddy Wayne's reach. After prepping the soldier's neck, Buddy Wayne had slathered it with a thick layer of acrylic glue. He held the head directly in front of his face and rotated it so that it was properly oriented in the same direction as the soldier's body. It was a delicate procedure, especially for someone who had only four and a half fingers. He then placed his elbows on the soldier's shoulders and slowly lowered the head into place. To his friends on the ground, the scene looked slightly romantic and they wondered if Buddy Wayne was about to give the head a kiss. He did not, and the head re-attached without incident.

When Buddy Wayne let go, he half expected the head to tumble to the earth. But it stayed put. The dark made it difficult to know for sure, but Buddy Wayne thought he had performed a perfect repair. He slid a trowel out of his tool belt and gingerly scraped away the glue that had oozed out beneath the soldier's jaw. For his final task, with the care of a mother bathing a newborn, he gently circled the PIMP's neck with a wet washcloth.

"I'm done," he announced as he started down the ladder.

"Reckon it's gonna hold?" asked John D.

"I think so," Buddy Wayne answered. "Maybe it'll last another 70 years, or at least 'til the next tornado."

The men lit another round of cigarettes and headed back to Frogeye's pickup.

"Mission accomplished," said Weaver.

"I heard that," said John D.

Day Seven

47. The National Guard Arrives

Saturday, March 13. 1982
6:00 a.m.
Paraclifta Hardware
Paraclifta, Arkansas

The members of the Consortium were in good spirits, but they were tired. It was rare for any of them to be awake past 10:00 p.m., and their statue repair had not been completed until after midnight.

It was Saturday the thirteenth and John D. was relieved that the thirteenth had not fallen on a Friday. He was not only incredibly superstitious, he also suffered from paraskevidekatriaphobia, the strong and irrational fear of Friday the 13th. One time, when the 13th fell on a Friday which was also the day after a full moon, he had refused to leave his house and cautiously walked around backwards the whole day. Other than the first week of deer season, that was the only time in two decades that Paraclifta Hardware had been closed on a weekday.

"I think we done a good job," said Buddy Wayne as he sipped his black coffee.

"Let's just hope it helps," said John D.

"It may not keep the *Foray* from showin' out, but if nothin' else, it oughta put an end to the debate over what to do with the PIMP," Buddy Wayne said.

"I reckon' Winthrop will be tickled when he figures out it's fixed," said Weaver.

"You'uns reckon they'll be a big crowd a folks at the courthouse this morning?" asked Frogeye.

"Probably." said Buddy Wayne. "Them *Foray* people put signs all over town advertisin' a rally. It ain't deer season and there ain't no football games to watch, so what else would anybody do today? I bet people'll drive in here from parts unknown hoping to see some kinda ruckus."

"The only way to get to Paraclifta is by driving. Y'all ever thought about that?" pondered Weaver. "We ain't got no airport and the river ain't big enough to get you nowhere."

"Reckon what's the best mode of travel that there is?" Frogeye asked.

"I'd say a pickup truck," offered Evelray. "It can carry you, and it can carry your stuff. Also, I ain't ridin' nothin' that ain't got brakes. There ain't no brakes on planes and ships."

The men ruminated on that topic for a half hour before they reached unanimous consent. Pickups were, in fact, the best mode of travel.

Around 7:30 a.m., the men thought they heard a freight train, which was ironic since they had been discussing transportation genres. They grabbed their cigarettes and walked to the front of the store to investigate. When they reached the plate-glass windows, they watched a convoy of Army transport trucks rumbling up Main Street. The National Guard had arrived.

48. The Big Demonstration

The Army trucks stopped at the courthouse square and the National Guardsmen disembarked in a semi-orderly fashion. The men had M-16 rifles slung over their shoulders and were carrying rectangular shields. They had wooden batons and see-through plastic visors draped from their helmets The scene reminded John D. of photographs of the troops at the notorious crisis when Little Rock Central High School was integrated in 1957. John D. and his friends were disheartened as they watched the soldiers take up positions around the courthouse.

"I can't believe this is happening here," said Weaver. "We're better than this."

"Reckon we should go down to the courthouse?" Buddy Wayne asked.

"Let's just stay in here and watch through the windows for now," John D. suggested.

A few minutes later, Frogeye pointed at the East End Eat, which was on the opposite side of the street. The café's employees and breakfast crowd had emptied onto the sidewalk. They were holding homemade signs that read: *We want head!*

Then the men craned their necks to look down the block on their own side of the street and saw that the Westside Diner's patrons and staff had also taken up a position on the opposite sidewalk. The Westside crowd, which included Molly the waitress, was standing behind a single large sign that was pointed toward the East End eaters. Because of their vantage point from inside the hardware store, the Consortium members could not identify what message was being conveyed by the Westsiders' sign.

"Son of a bitch," said Evelray. "Them diners may finally get to the lick log."

Frogeye shifted nervously from one leg to the other. He was glad that he was situated on the west side of the street. He knew that if violence erupted, his loyalty would require him to join the Westsiders. He looked back across the street and said, "Damn. I'm sad and surprised to see the Chinquapin Lady over there with the East Enders."

Sure enough, the Chinquapin Lady was standing with the opposing crowd. She had her burial box cradled in her left arm while her right arm held a sign that read, *Head Yes!*

During the café confrontation, Winthrop was walking through the back door of the courthouse. He was pushing his Paw-Paw in a wheelchair. Even though J.D. was still ambulatory, he was riding in the wheelchair since it was his idea to include *a cripple* in today's operations. So far, the arrangement had worked out swimmingly because Winthrop was glad to have his Paw-Paw close by for consultation and J.D. was enjoying being pushed around.

The Paraclifta courthouse had the only elevator in the county. It was a good thing, because eight years later, Congress would pass the Americans with Disabilities Act, which would have required that one be installed. Congressman Kochran would eventually vote against the Americans with Disabilities Act. He believed that it was an unnecessary government overreach that had been concocted by communists.

Winthrop rolled J.D.'s wheelchair into the elevator and they patiently waited for it to deliver them to the second floor. The trip took four minutes. J.D. smoked one and a half cigarettes during the ascent.

When Winthrop finally reached his office, he found that Dorinda was already there and was busy rehearsing her comments for the upcoming ceremony. J.D. continued smoking the last half of the cigarette he had started on the elevator and took a minute to admire Dorinda's figure. Then he looked up at Winthrop, pointed at Dorinda's bottom, and said, "How 'bout you let that fine-lookin' woman take over the wheelchair maneuvering?"

"OK with me," said Winthrop.

Winthrop left J.D. and Dorinda in the lobby and took refuge in his private office. He figured that most everyone in town knew his Paw-Paw and he thought it would be a nice touch to have the oldest man in the county next to him at the podium, even if he was sitting in a wheel chair.

As he looked out the windows at the National Guard troops, he spotted Toehead and the football team strolling confidently up Main Street. He could see the café customers on both sides of the street and they appeared to be cheering and holding up signs for the boys. *Now that's a nice touch,* he thought.

Then he saw a phalanx of reporters jostling for position outside the courthouse. For the third time in a week, the media had descended on Paraclifta. Winthrop knew that reporters were going to ask for his thoughts about POOPIE and PEE PEE, but he was still not sure how he would respond. He just wanted the outsiders to go home and then he could figure out how to fix the statue of his great-great grandfather. *There should not be a headless PIMP on the court-house lawn,* he thought. *Couldn't everyone at least agree with that?*

Down on Main Street, the members of the Consortium were excited to see Toehead and the team, so they decided to exit the hardware store so they could clap when the players passed by.

"That's a good-lookin' bunch," observed John D. as he clapped.

"Shore are," said Frogeye, "and they're're gonna beat Paraloma's ass this season."

The football team stopped at the ruins of the pharmacy store and waited for instructions. One of the volunteer firemen met them and opened a box of surgical masks that had been dug out of the rubble.

The fireman looked at Toehead and said, "Coach, you should have the boys wear these things. It's mighty dusty up in there, on account of all the asbestos."

Toehead barked out some instructions and the players lined up, slapped on face masks and started hauling debris to a des-ignated area next to a county dump truck parked behind the store. The masked players moved swiftly and efficiently, like a swarm of worker bees, as they hauled out bricks, boxes and busted furniture.

At 9:15, a group of inmates began preparing a make-shift stage for Winthrop's presentation. A podium and flags were erected at the top of the courthouse steps and the inmates took duct tape and cordoned off a swath of the lawn between the steps and Main Street. Luckily, Dicey Davidson was there. He announced that the tape covered an area that was forty feet longwise and twenty-five feet crosswise. This area was the demilitarized zone and Winthrop had ordered the National Guard to prevent any unauthorized persons, particularly *Foray* members, from having access thereto. The soldiers watched the area warily and looked like they were keen on protecting it.

At 9:20, a caravan of menacing-looking pickups with out-of-state license plates slowly inched its way up Main Street. The trucks, which were occupied by *Foray* members, took up all the remaining parking spots near the courthouse. The *Foray* members, who were all wearing facemasks, disembarked and mustered up near the edge of the courthouse square.

A few minutes before the planned announcement, Winthrop stepped onto the courthouse landing. He was soon joined by the newest pastor in town. A moment later, Dorinda wheeled J.D. up to the podium. Winthrop had given some big speeches, but he had never been more nervous. He stood at the podium and fumbled with his notes as the television cameras began to film the scene.

When it appeared that the ceremony was about to commence, a hush fell over the crowd on the courthouse lawn. Just before Winthrop was ready to introduce the pastor, J.D. turned in his wheel chair to eyeball his dad's statue. Then, the oldest man in the county sprang from the chair, thrust his arms in the air and yelled, "Pappy's got his head fixed!"

This caused Winthrop to whip around and gaze at the statue. "Hallelujah … Glory Hallelujah!" he exclaimed into the microphone. Then he turned back around and saw J.D. in a passionate embrace with Dorinda.

Meanwhile the folks in the crowd, many of whom were already predisposed to start trouble, were trying to get a handle on what in the world was going on. They had just seen a feeble old white man jump out of a wheelchair and start hugging an attractive young black woman while the Judge was screaming *Hallelujah!* In a matter of seconds, someone in the crowd realized that the PIMP's head had been re-attached and pointed at the statue. News of the head's reappearance spread through the crowd like a salacious rumor, and the onlookers began to cheer and clap.

The resulting commotion led the football players to halt their cleanup efforts and they walked out to the sidewalk in front of the ruined drug store. When the *Foray* members saw the football players' face coverings, they quickly concluded that the boys were fellow members, so they headed that direction.

Suddenly, and without warning, the high school marching band, *the Pride of Paraclifta*, emerged at the far end of south Main

Street. They were in full formation and marching straight toward the courthouse. Not only had Toehead organized the football team, he had also asked the band to march up to the courthouse to coincide with Winthrop's announcement. The marching band was blaring the school's fight song, *When the PIMPs Come Marching Home*. The song was played to the tune of *When the Saints Go Marching In*.

Instinctively, all of the Paraclifta residents began to clap to the song's rhythm while singing its lyrics:

Oh When the PIMPs, come marching home,
Oh when the PIMPs, come marching home,
I want to be in that number,
When the PIMPs come marching home.

Oh when the sun, begins to shine,
We know the PIMPs, are feelin' fine
I want to be in that number,
When the PIMPs come marching home.

Oh, when the PIMPs, come marching home,
From Mississip' to Oklahoma,
We know those PIMPs, will come back home.
In time to watch us beat Paraloma.

When the band reached the destroyed drug store, the football players and the *Foray* members joined in and marched behind. All of them had their arms in the air with their index fingers pointed toward the sky. The football players were giving the *number one* sign because they believed they were the best team in the state. The *Foray* members were doing so because it was their special sign. Many people on the sidewalks (those who were not clapping rhythmically) also gave the *number one* sign.

Then, something truly astonishing occurred. The crowds from each of the diners merged behind the band and mask-wearing marchers and shook hands. They threw down their competing NO-HEAD and NEW-HEAD signs and joined the procession.

From the podium on the courthouse square, Winthrop grinned and began singing the fight song as the band drew near. By this time, the news media had scattered in several directions. Some were filming the Paraclifta band, some were taking photographs of the repaired Rebel statue and others were focused on J.D., who had yet to stop hugging Dorinda.

In perfect formation, the band halted on the courthouse lawn. And once again, a hush fell over the crowd. Still a bit unsure about what all had happened, Winthrop leaned into the microphone.

"Friends," he said, "The first thing I'd like to do is ask Brother Waymon to say a few words"

After the newest pastor in town provided a very nice prayer, everyone said, *amen.*

Winthrop returned to the podium. He pointed at the statue and said, "Ladies and Gentlemen, as you can see, we ain't got no problem. The PIMP got his head back!"

The crowd roared with approval.

Winthrop pointed at the marching band. "Now, let's give a big hand to the *Pride of Paraclifta.*"

When the cheering abated, Winthrop pointed to the boys wearing masks. As he did so, he thought that it must be the largest number of football players the town had ever produced. *I can't believe we got that many boys on the team this year.* "And, how about a hand for our football boys!"

The players and the *Foray* members all gave the number one sign to the clapping crowd. Then the crowd began to chant, *"Beat Paraloma ... Beat Paraloma ..."*

The *Foray* members had no idea what was going on, but they enjoyed it immensely. None of them had ever played football or received joyful cheers from strangers.

As the cheering continued, Coach Toehead Faulkner walked up to the podium and asked Winthrop for permission to make an announcement. Then he took the microphone and addressed the crowd.

"Folks, my football boys and the band are honored to be here today."

His remarks were interrupted by someone who shouted, "Beat Paraloma!"

"You can count on that," replied Toehead. "But right now, my boys are gonna keep working to help with the storm cleanup and we'd like to invite ever body else to join in. Then, around noon, the Booster Club parents and several of the Baptist churches are gonna set up a free picnic."

When Toehead set down the microphone, the crowd screamed its approval again while the band lit into yet another round of the fight song. At the end of the song, the crowd dispersed and everyone, including the press and the National Guardsmen, began cleaning up on Main Street. For the next two hours, hundreds of people cooperated to haul off debris from the damaged businesses. All of them happily wore masks, except when they stopped to eat, drink or smoke a cigarette.

The band members laid down their instruments and helped carry catalpa limbs off the courthouse lawn. They were aided by the county inmates and the members of the Consortium.

Even though he was out on bail, Junior Smitherton was also helping the inmates. At one point, he and Weaver were able to have a nice conversation and exchanged gardening ideas.

During the morning, workers from the East End Eat and the Westside Diner roamed amongst the volunteers passing out treats. They gave out blueberry muffins, cat-head biscuits, pinwheel rolls, jalapeno cornbread, deep-fried hush puppies and chocolate chip cookies. Frogeye, like many of his neighbors, was amazed that the food from both cafés tasted identical.

As the clean-up carried on, Dicey Davidson took an immeasurable number of measurements, securing lengths and widths of everything from Army trucks to musical instruments while the Chinquapin Lady meandered around the courthouse square, fiercely grasping her burial box, muttering about space lasers.

By lunchtime, all of the detritus from the storm had been removed from the drug store and the service station. Anyone just arriving in town would have been clueless that a tornado had smashed through just a week ago.

The Booster Club parents and the ladies from the Baptist churches (which turned out to be all the same people) set up four rows of tables and laid table cloths and quilts all over the courthouse square. The tables were loaded with pan-fried chicken, smoked ham, and pimento cheese sandwiches on white bread. They had potato chips, potato salad, hash brown casseroles, deviled eggs and baked beans. They also had a plethora of pies.

Not to be outdone, the Paraclifta Volunteer Fire Department had also sprung into action. While the department had never been adept at fighting fires, they were undefeated when it came to throwing a barbecue. Their members also set up a serving station on the lawn, offering baby back ribs and pulled pork sandwiches. They normally sold these items as a fundraiser twice a year, but today they were handing them out for free, while making it clear that they were happy to accept any donations since many of them had been involved in the multi-vehicle pile-up after responding to the tornado.

Around noon, everyone lined up at the tables and fixed their plates. Soon, the courthouse lawn was a sea of harmonious humanity as inmates and deputies, soldiers and civilians, football players and band nerds, preachers and sinners, Blacks and whites, and customers from rival cafes, all dined in peace.

The members of the Consortium were sitting together on a blanket in the shadow of the PIMP. John D. took off his mask and was about to attack his plate of homemade vittles when he looked at his friends and said, "Wow. This is something I never thought I'd see."

"Me neither," said Frogeye. "The Volunteer Fire Department giving their pulled-pork sandwiches away for free."

"No, you dumbass," said John D. "All these different kinds of people sittin' around in harmony, enjoyin' each other's company."

"Oh," said Frogeye.

"Well, things couldn't a turnt out no better," Weaver observed. "Nobody's bitchin' about the statue, ever body's happy, and Junior's not gonna have to go to jail."

"I heard that," said Buddy Wayne.

At that moment, Dorinda and one-hundred-and-seven-year-old J.D. Hatfield were the only people not sitting on the courthouse lawn. That was only because J.D. had returned to his wheelchair and Dorinda was pushing him around, from group to group, so he could visit with them all.

At 12:30, the band members retrieved their instruments and played the fight song one more time while the crowd stood and sang along. Nobody took time to look at the Rebel PIMP, who was standing tall and gazing over the entire crowd of perfectly-content Americans. Nobody. It was too bad. Because at that moment, it appeared that the face on the statue was smiling and had a tear in its eye.

Epilogue

The men of the Consortium never told anyone that they were the ones who fixed the head on the Confederate statue.

As predicted by Buddy Wayne Pike, the catalpa trees at the Paraclifta courthouse rebounded nicely after the tornado. They are still beautiful in the spring.

Each year, on the first Saturday after the first full moon in March, the city of Paraclifta hosts a celebration called the *Spring Fling*. At 11:00 in the morning, the courthouse warning sirens are activated to signal the start of a parade down Main Street. The parade is led by the *Pride of Paraclifta* marching band followed by the football team. The parade also includes several floats, a couple of National Guard vehicles and dozens of siren-clad pickups driven by the volunteer firemen. It ends at the courthouse square, where everyone dons face coverings and sings the high school fight song before enjoying a fine picnic. It is one of the biggest local events of the year, along with the first day of deer season and the high school football game against Paraloma. Many elected officials and political candidates make sure to attend. It closely resembles the spontaneous celebration that took place in 1982, except that the volunteer fire department now charges for their food.

The *Foray* disbanded four years later, but its members had so much fun in Paraclifta that many of them continued to attend the *Spring Fling.*

After leaving Paraclifta, Quincy "Q-AN" Nguyen was never seen again. According to rumors, he relocated in a wet county somewhere in the Northeast where he began making up crazy conspiracy theories.

When the global Coronavirus pandemic struck the planet in 2020, Paraclifta was ok. The folks there were accustomed to wearing masks and had no reason to resist officials who recommended it. Of course, they continued to remove their masks to eat, drink or smoke a cigarette.

When it convened for the 1983 Regular Session, the Arkansas General Assembly declined to consider Cammack Cafflin's bill. The state legislature had bigger fish to fry, like passing a law to make school teachers take a series of tests in order to keep their license to teach. They hoped that this would lead to smarter students.

Congressman Finius Kochran's legislation never became the law either. Federal legislators decided that they had better things to do than to worry about statues at county courthouses. But things weren't all bad for Finius. WASTE's decision to have federal facilities switch from regular bars of soap to liquid soap in plastic dispensers made a fortune for his friends at PMS. And, in 1983, the tax cuts he had included in PEE PEE came to pass anyway after Congress approved another reduction in the highest personal income tax rate.

John D. was right about the Chinquapin Lady. She had gone off the deep end and had to be sent to the crazy house. The folks in Paraclifta believed that institutionalization was the only appropriate way to deal with someone who believed in Jewish space lasers.

Junior Smitherton successfully completed his probation for drug possession. He never had any more trouble with the law and his conviction was expunged in 2001. Fifteen years later, voters in the state of Arkansas legalized the use of marijuana for *medical* purposes and in 2017, Junior obtained a marijuana cultivation license which authorized him to become a commercial grower. Relying on the gardening advice he had received from Weaver Gillham, Junior's company, *Foray Farms*, eventually became the largest marijuana distributor in the state.

In 1993, a new monument was placed on the opposite side of the Paraclifta courthouse. It was a veterans' memorial wall containing the name of every county resident who died in any of the nation's armed conflicts since 1900. It has 162 names, including the names of J.D. Hatfield's son and grandson. The most recent name was added in 2019 when a Paraclifta High School graduate who was serving in the Marine Corps was killed in the desolate mountains of Afghanistan.

The statue of Nahem Hatfield still stands on the courthouse grounds with a head that looks down Main Street. Nobody really pays much attention to it. Nobody. The plaque on the statue still says: THE PRINCIPLES FOR WHICH THEY FOUGHT LIVE ETERNALLY. But if there is one eternal principle that the people of Paraclifta understand it is this—*Pimpin' ain't easy.*

About the Author

Thule Taaffe is a seventh-generation Arkansan. This is his second novel about the Paraclifta Consortium. Visit **purplehullpress.com**. for information about his upcoming novels and his previous book, *Milk and Catfish*.

www.ingramcontent.com/pod-product-compliance
Lightning Source LLC
Chambersburg PA
CBHW051134020726
47501CB00005B/1508